Stella Díaz Has Something to Say

I do!

STELLA DÍAZ HAS Something to SAY

ANGELA DOMINGUEZ

SQUARE FISH

Roaring Brook Press
New York

SQUARE FISH

An imprint of Macmillan Publishing Group, LLC
175 Fifth Avenue, New York, NY 10010
mackids.com

Library of Congress Control Number: 2017944674

ISBN 978-1-250-29410-4 (paperback)   ISBN 978-1-62672-859-2 (ebook)

Originally published in the United States by Roaring Brook Press
First Square Fish edition, 2019
Book design by Elizabeth H. Clark
Square Fish logo designed by Filomena Tuosto

7   9   10   8

AR:4.2 / LEXILE: 650L

To Mom, Connie,
Linda, and everyone
who inspired this story

Chapter One

The smell of *albóndigas* fills the house when my brother, Nick, and I come home.

"Time for our weekly appointment," says Nick, walking in the direction of the kitchen.

I nod. My mouth starts to water as I follow him toward the sound of sizzling food.

Around the corner, I see Mom performing her magic over a large pot on the stove. Her eyes are closed as she carefully tastes some tomato sauce with a wooden spoon. She's still wearing her work clothes except she has an apron on and slippers instead of high heels. Mom works every day in an office, which means she can't make dinner weeknights except for

Fridays, better known as our "weekly appointment." It's also the night we play board games past our regular bedtime.

"*¡Mis bebés!*" Mom exclaims when she sees us. She spreads her arms wide to give us big hugs and kisses.

"Can I help, Mom?" I ask, wiping lipstick off my cheek.

"Of course, Stella! Do you want to boil the e-spaghetti while I go change *mi ropa*?" She tugs at her clothes and takes off her apron.

I say, "*¡Síííííííííííí!*" but inside I giggle.

While Mom speaks both English and Spanish perfectly, strangers say she has an accent. To me, it's just the way she speaks. Although every once in a while I can hear that she says a word a little funny, like "e-spaghetti."

When Mom returns to the kitchen, she's wearing an oversized shirt and jeans instead of her business suit. She leans over the pot of simmering *albóndigas*, wiggles her nose, and takes a deep sniff. Mom says that you can always smell when the food is ready. She looks at me as she gives me the thumbs-up.

"Stella, grab the *platos, por favor*," says Mom.

I put the plates on the table while Nick helps Mom carry the food. She scoops some e-spaghetti and *albóndigas* onto my plate. While she passes it to me, she makes sure to pull off the bay leaf. Mom says the bay leaf gives the *albóndigas* their extra *sabor*, but we shouldn't eat it. Nick serves himself. Mom still likes to treat me like the baby even though I'm in third grade.

As soon as we start eating together, Mom asks, "So how was your week at school, *niños*?"

Nick starts talking right away as he twirls his e-spaghetti on his fork. "Pretty good. I think I'm going to join the basketball team this year. Jason and Adam are joining, too." Nick is in eighth grade, and the middle school kids get to play sports.

Mom smiles. "You're going to get so strong!"

Nick blushes. "Yeah. Plus it's going to make it even easier to beat Stella at arm wrestling."

"I'll just practice more," I say, and stick out my tongue at him.

Mom doesn't get mad. She rarely does. She only gets mad when there is hair pulling or name calling, which doesn't happen too often. She also won't take sides, as much as I want her to sometimes. Instead, she just laughs it off. "What about you, Stella? How was your week?"

"Amazing. Today Ms. Bell said we are going to start sustained reading in class. That means we just get to read quietly. I think I'm going to read about fishes because of Pancho," I say.

Mom says, "That sounds fun. I bet Pancho is going to appreciate it."

Pancho is my betta fish. That is a type of fish that likes to be alone.

They can be as colorful as the rainbow, but Pancho is mostly blue, which is my favorite color. I like that Pancho likes to be alone and is okay being quiet.

Mom winks at me. "Anything else?"

"Oh, Ms. Bell also said we are going to have a new student next week. I hope it's a girl so she can play with Jenny and me. It's hard to play tag when it's only two people," I say while I slurp up a noodle.

"Well, I'm certain whoever it is, they will be nice. Just be sure to make them feel comfortable and be my sweet Stella," she says.

I nod my head. "Promise."

Mom has no idea how excited I am about the new student. School has been a little lonely without my best friend, Jenny, in my class. I've been trying hard to make more friends, but it's not so easy. The first day of class especially didn't go so well this year. I could barely talk because my stomach was in knots all day. Then when I did talk, I messed up. I had to read aloud a paragraph I wrote about my summer break, and I said some of the words wrong. That made some of the kids in my class, like Jessica Anderson, laugh.

I hope the new kid is a girl who's a lot like me. Maybe she loves to draw or has a fish, too, or can run fast like me. I'm sure she might be a little lonely or scared on her first day like I was. I'm sure she'll appreciate my help. I'll show her the tricks around the school, like which lunch lady gives extra French fries or which bathrooms aren't as nice.

I look over at Nick.

"Did you learn anything cool today?" It's one of my favorite things to ask him at dinner. Everything you get to learn in eighth grade just seems really interesting.

He thinks for a second. "Well, we studied tornadoes and all types of weather in science. The videos were pretty cool."

"Tornadoes?! They're scary! Wait . . . can they happen in Chicago, Nick?"

He starts to snicker. Whenever he snickers, I know he is up to no good.

6

"Yes," he says. "*Tomatoes* can happen in Chicago."

I cross my arms. "Ugh, Nick! You know I said 'tornadoes,' not 'tomatoes.'"

"I heard 'tomatoes,' and you shouldn't be afraid of them." Then he gently elbows me. "Now *Brussels sprouts*, those *are* scary."

"Guess I'm making Brussels sprouts next Friday," says Mom, winking at me.

Nick groans, "Eww. Okay. No more vegetable talk."

Nick is pretty stellar most of the time, but he can still be an annoying older brother sometimes. Nick knows it especially bothers me that he laughs when I mess up my words. I can't help it. Sometimes I mix up the way words or letters sound, and when I do I turn *roja* like a tomato. That's because the letters sound a little different in English and Spanish. I'm taking a class to help me, but I don't like that I have to take it, and I definitely don't like people making fun of me.

Chapter Two

We eat until my stomach is as round as an *albóndiga*. Then we move to the living room to play cards. Mom puts on salsa music and we always end up dancing around the room. That's different from chips and salsa. It's a dance where you sometimes do a dip, but mostly you shake your hips and twirl around. It's really fun.

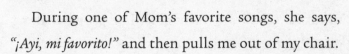

During one of Mom's favorite songs, she says, *"¡Ayi, mi favorito!"* and then pulls me out of my chair.

I wouldn't even dream of dancing at school, but with Mom it is so fun.

"Stella, we used to dance to this song when we lived in Mexico City," she says as she spins me around.

"How?!" My family is from Mexico, but we moved to Chicago when I was a baby. I can't picture a baby dancing. I don't even know any babies who dance. They can barely walk!

"Well, *technically* I rocked you in my arms, but I danced enough for the two of us."

Mom picks me up for a second like I'm a baby, and it makes me laugh. Then she tries to pick up Nick, but he groans, "Mom!" As he brushes his hair back, I notice the smallest smirk on his right cheek. Lately, Nick is acting like he is too old to play with us, but I know he secretly still likes being silly. The smirk always gives it away.

After many rounds of cards and salsa dancing, I head up to my room. Before bed, I feed my betta fish. "Next week, I'm going to learn everything about you and your relatives, Pancho," I say.

Then I crawl into bed and stare at him swimming. I love Pancho, but I'm really glad I'm not a betta fish. I couldn't be in a tank all by myself, without my family. I giggle. Nick would look funny as a talking fish. As I close my eyes, I start picturing the new student and my future friend. "I hope she speaks Spanish," I say as I drift off to sleep.

Chapter Three

Monday morning, Nick walks me to my school before he heads over to Arlington Heights Middle School.

He is about to say his usual "Bye, sis," when Jenny runs over. She has a huge smile, and then she twists around. I see why she's so happy. She has a new backpack, and it has glitter, sparkles, and a cat. It's *very* Jenny.

"Like it?" she asks.

"*Yes!*" I say.

"Thanks! I wanted to get one that looks like Anna's."

"Who???" I ask.

"Anna. She's in my class. She has the best taste."
Jenny grins.

Nick rolls his eyes. "Girls." He *does not* like sparkles. Then he rubs my head and takes off as Jenny and I walk into our school.

"I almost forgot," Jenny says. "I have lychee candy for you. My mom went to the Vietnamese market."

She opens her backpack to give me the candy. I lick my lips.

Jenny's family is from Vietnam, but, unlike me, Jenny was born here in Chicago.

"Yum!" I say, popping a piece in my mouth.

Jenny nods and looks into her classroom. "Oh, I see Anna. I have to show her my new backpack. See you at lunch, Stella!"

The backpack that looks like Anna's bounces as Jenny runs into the room. From where I am standing, I can see Jenny talking to Anna, but only the back of Anna's head.

Who is this Anna? I think to myself.

I sigh and look down at the best-friend bracelet Jenny gave me over the summer. It suddenly looks smaller than usual, especially compared to a backpack. I'm glad Jenny isn't lonely in her class, but she and I are the only ones who are supposed to match. If there was a rule book to being best friends, I'm sure rules on matching would be in the top ten, easily. It's just part of being best friends.

Luckily, I start feeling better as soon as I get to my room and see Ms. Bell standing in front of the whiteboard. She's wearing polka dots again.

"They're my favorite," she told us on the first day of class, which made me happy. Polka dots are my favorite, too.

I sit down in my assigned seat as Ms. Bell carefully starts to write our agenda for the day on the board. In perfect cursive handwriting, she squiggles:

1. Library Visit
2. Sustained Reading
3. Lunch
4. Storytime
5. Science

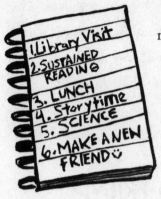

I copy it down in my spiral notebook. Then I add a sixth item to my schedule and draw a smiley face: "Make a New Friend." Today is going to be a good day.

"Ms. Bell, are you going to read from *Help! I'm a Prisoner in the Library* again today after lunch?" asks Chris Pollard. He's one of the loudest kids in our class and is best friends with Ben Shaw, the class clown.

"Seems only appropriate since we're visiting the library this morning, doesn't it?" she says as she pushes her glasses up the bridge of her nose.

Hearing that makes me feel happy. Even though we can all read really well, Ms. Bell reads out loud to us a little bit every day during storytime. It's just one chapter, but it's like watching a play. I close my eyes, remembering how Ms. Bell does all these great voices for all the characters.

Suddenly the bell rings. I open my eyes. The classroom is full except for the one empty seat where the new kid (aka my new friend) will sit. I bet she will have the best taste. Even better than Anna's.

NEW FRIEND

Chapter Four

Ms. Morales is standing by the front door of the library to greet us one by one when we arrive for today's library visit. She is wearing her long pearls and a bright orange sweater, and on her left arm she's holding her stuffed goose named Lucy, which everyone gets to honk when they leave the library.

"*Hola, Stella,*" Ms. Morales says.

"*¡Buenos días, Ms. Morales!*" I say quietly, but I squeal inside.

Ms. Morales has been our librarian since kindergarten. The best thing about Ms. Morales, apart from the fact that she speaks Spanish, is that she's so smart and loves sharing books with us. At the beginning of this year, when I started getting interested in fishes, she showed me all these books on Jacques Cousteau, a famous ocean explorer. Now I love reading about him.

"Welcome, Ms. Bell's class!" she announces as soon as all of us are sitting in front of a computer. Ms. Morales is full of spunk and a little different from your usual librarian. I think most librarians don't have purple streaks in their hair.

Instead of saying hello back, we wave our hands in the air. Ms. Morales says proper library etiquette calls for no loud voices.

Ms. Morales waves back and continues, "I hear you are all finding books for your sustained reading. Now, you remember how to use the catalog, right? Just find the Dewey decimal number, write it down, and look for the book on the shelf. If you have any questions, I am here!"

The Dewey decimal system is how the books are organized at the library. If it were up to me, I would just organize them by color like my colored pencils or by height like my books at home. Still, it really does help when searching for books. With the power of Dewey, I find the *perfecto* book.

I grab it and head over to a big table by myself. The pictures are so beautiful. I want to dog-ear the pages, but I only do that to my books at home. Ms. Bell comes up to me, crouches down, and says in a quiet voice, "What book are you reading, Stella?"

"*What Lives in the Ocean?* by Tonya Mickelson," I say quietly.

"Sounds positively fascinating!" she whispers.

"It is. Did you know

that an octopus doesn't have any bones and has three hearts? I have to draw it later. It's just too cool-looking."

"I heard an octopus named Paul became famous for predicting many of the winners of the World Cup."

"Wow!" I exclaim.

Ms. Bell chuckles. She lifts her fingers to her mouth. When I get excited, I speak louder than I realize.

"I think there will be a little time for drawing after the library," she whispers before standing.

I smile and keep reading about octopuses. It turns out they are extraordinary escape artists. To escape from their enemies, they release a cloud of ink to help them disappear. Then, because they have no bones, they can maneuver through almost any nook or cranny. They can even escape through a hole only an inch wide! That would be a really helpful skill to have.

When it's time to go back to class, everyone says goodbye to Ms. Morales and Lucy.

"*Adiós*, Ms. Morales and Lucy," I say as I give the stuffed goose a squeeze. I have to admit, even though I'm in third grade and too old for this, it's still sort of fun.

Lucy honks, and Ms. Morales and I both smile. "*Hasta luego, Stella.*"

When we get back to the room, everyone starts chatting about their books, except for me. I get started drawing my octopus. I'm about halfway finished, making sure I draw all eight arms the same size, when I hear a knock on the door. I look up and Ms. Green, who works in the office, is at the door. Ms. Bell meets her and whispers.

I hear Ben Shaw say to Chris Pollard, "It must be the new kid."

I drop my colored pencils. I got so carried away with the library and my drawing that I almost forgot. Then I see who is standing next to Ms. Green. It's a boy! And he has light brown hair. I frown a little. That's very different from what I imagined.

"Class," Ms. Bell says, "this is our new student. Do you want to introduce yourself to the class?"

The new boy waves at everyone, and says, "Howdy! I'm Stanley Mason. I just moved here from Dallas, Texas, or *Tejas en español.*"

Ms. Bell says, "*Tejas!* That's so far away from here. Has anyone been to Texas?"

A few kids raise their hands. I actually was in Texas last year on our family road trip. We went to see the Alamo and we even went to a cave where we took a picture with a dinosaur sculpture named

Grendel. But I'm always too shy to speak up in class. Plus, the Alamo isn't in Dallas. Stanley probably hasn't even seen it. Still, even if I weren't shy, I wouldn't be able to talk right now. I'm a little speechless. I can't believe Stanley speaks *español*! He doesn't look like someone who would speak Spanish at all. The new kid I imagined had dark brown hair like me and not light hair. And she was a girl.

Ms. Bell says, "Now, class, let's have everyone quickly introduce yourself to Stanley."

One by one, people stand. There are about ten people in front of me, and I feel nervous and a little sweaty. I want to make a new friend so badly, even if he is a boy. So what if he is not at all the girl I had pictured in my head? He speaks Spanish like me, and, more important, he's new. He could use a friend as much as I could. I could be his first new friend here.

When it's my turn, I stand up. I feel myself turning *roja*. I freeze. I just read that some octopuses can paralyze their prey. Maybe Stanley is part octopus.

Probably not. He looks like a normal boy with freckles, blue eyes, and a cool monkey shirt. I catch myself staring at him for a second.

"Hmm . . . *me llamo Stella,*" I say while looking away quickly. "Sorry, I mean I'm Stella." I say it even faster as I sit back down. I'm about to groan out of embarrassment when I feel my chair start to tilt backward. My eyes grow *grande* like an elephant, and everything slows down. I try to reach out to grab my desk, but it's too late.

Crash!

Before I know it, my feet are sticking straight up in the air, and my back is on the ground. I've fallen down in front of Stanley—in front of everyone! I close my eyes as I hear the entire class laugh.

I check my arms and legs. Nothing hurts. I think about staying on the ground but decide to crawl up. I poke my eyes above my desk.

"Are you okay, Stella?" Ms. Bell is the only one not laughing.

"Yes," I whisper.

I look at Stanley. He looks like he wants to laugh, but he is holding it in. *There goes my new friend*, I think. *Who would want a klutz for a friend?*

I pull my chair back up and sit down. On top of it, I can't believe I spoke Spanish instead of English. *Doubly embarrassing.*

I stare at my drawing and think about escaping through a tiny hole. Or disappearing in a cloud of ink. Today, I really wish I were an octopus.

Chapter Five

"Want a cookie? It has M&M's in it, Stella. Do you like M&M's?"

I'm in the middle of drawing sea creatures during class, but I immediately stop what I'm doing to consider the question.

Oooo . . . I do like M&M's, I think.

I look up, dropping my pink colored pencil.

It's Stanley.

Stanley Mason.

He is holding a box full of cookies. It's been a few weeks and I've managed not to speak to him once

since falling down on his first day of class. I've just
been too embarrassed. Even so, it's impolite to refuse
a cookie, so I nod and grab one. My hand is shaking
as I take a bite.

"My mom made them for my birthday." Stanley
grins widely. I notice he has a gap between his front
two teeth.

"Oh . . . Happy birthday," I mumble.

As I chew, I notice little cookie crumbs and spit fall all over my shirt. I cover my mouth with my hand so I don't look like a total disaster.

"Thanks, Stella. What are you drawing?"

I shake my head no. I use my cookie-free hand to flip over my drawing. I was trying to draw a blobfish, but it just looks like a pink mess. This will not be the first thing Stanley sees me draw. I only let people look at my drawings when they are perfect.

"Oh, okay," he says with a frown.

I'm surprised. Why would he care? It's not like he wants to be friends with a klutz like me.

I feel a little bad, so I mumble, "Thank you for the cookie," with my hand over my mouth again. Stanley looks happy. He opens his mouth as if he is about to say something else.

Luckily, Ms. Bell says, "Everyone sit down."

"Stanley, come sit by us," says Jessica Anderson while Ben Shaw and Chris Pollard wave him over.

I watch Stanley take his seat next to them. My mouth drops open. I'm amazed. In just a couple of weeks, he fits in already! I don't get it. Stanley also has not once looked sad or scared. Not even for a second! If I had moved to a new city and school, I'd be terrified.

Ms. Bell continues, "In just a little bit we are going to have a special ceremony for Don. Now everyone knows Don, right?"

"Don's the coolest!" says Ben Shaw.

Everyone agrees. Don, the school custodian, is always singing fun Beach Boys songs while he's cleaning. He also plays the craziest characters in the school plays, like Santa Claus in our holiday musical.

"Well, Don just became an American citizen, which is really hard! You have to take a big test. Not to mention all the years of waiting."

Jessica Anderson asks, "What was he before?"

Ms. Bell goes up to the board. She writes a bunch of words I haven't heard before. In big letters, I see "visa," "alien," "resident," and "citizen." "Great question. There are a few categories. Some people just come to visit. They get a piece of paper called a visa so they can stay awhile."

"Don't you buy things with a visa?" asks Jessica. I lock eyes with her for a second, then quickly look away. Although I've been in the same class with Jessica since first grade, she makes me nervous. Everyone likes her, but I think she can be mean sometimes. Like when she laughed at me the first day of class for saying words wrong. Then another time, in first grade, she told everyone in our class that I had lice. Everyone believed her except for Jenny. The teacher even made me see the school nurse. And of course, I didn't have lice. Afterward, Jessica said she was sorry, but I never quite believed her.

Ms. Bell chuckles. "Yes, you do, but that's a different visa. For instance, people who come here for college get a student visa so they can stay here the entire time they are going to school.

"Then there are residents or legal aliens. They have green cards. They can stay here as long as they want, but they don't have as many rights as citizens."

My mouth drops open. I only have a green card. I know because Mom showed it to me when we got it in the mail. I was surprised that it wasn't green at all. I don't know too much about how we got it. I remember Mom was really stressed about it. I also remember waiting in line forever. The only part that was fun was getting fingerprints done. Oh, and taking bunches of pictures for it. But still, because of this green card, I'm an *alien*?

Ms. Bell continues, "After you've been a resident for a while you can apply to be a citizen. Then you can vote and be on a jury. You can even run for office!"

"What if you were born here?" asks Michelle.

"Then you're already a citizen. A natural citizen."

I gulp again. This explains everything. I'm an alien!

"Since Don works so hard for us, we're going to surprise him with a celebration in the cafeteria!" Ms. Bell continues. "We're all going to go quietly and sit in the dark until Don arrives. Then we'll turn on the lights, stand up, and sing 'The Star-Spangled Banner.' Don't worry, we will have a projector with the words for you to sing along with. If you guys do well, there might be cake."

Everyone squeals but me. I always thought I was different, that I didn't really belong. But now it's official.

I start picturing all the aliens I've seen in movies, trying to find one that isn't so strange. If I could picture only one cute alien, I might feel better about the word. Instead, as we head out to the cafeteria, I picture all these spiny, crawly, deadly aliens, the ones people run away from.

When we arrive, I notice that the orchestra is on the stage. There are also some banners that read "Way to Go!" and "Congrats!"

Because the whole school is there, I'm able to sit next to Jenny. I feel calmer when I see her, except she's not alone. She's sitting next to a girl I've never seen before. The new girl has bangs that go across her forehead and is wearing neat red glasses. My heart sinks a little. I want to tell Jenny the bad news that I'm an alien, but I can't. Not in front of the new girl.

"Stella, this is Anna," says Jenny.

"Hi, Stella," Anna says, waving.

I make myself wave back. "Did you guys know about the ceremony?" I ask in a low voice.

"What did she say?" asks Anna, looking at Jenny.

"Stella asked if we knew about the ceremony," says Jenny.

Jenny can always understand me. It's been that way since we became best friends in first grade. Never have I ever had to repeat anything to her once.

They turn and both nod at me. Then there's a long silence. There is so much that I want to say to Jenny, but I can't. Even if Anna weren't there, it would be too embarrassing to say out loud.

Just then the school nurse walks by and says, "Here you are, girls," as she gives us small flags to hold.

A minute later the cafeteria goes dark. The whole group giggles for a second, and the teachers hush us. We wait in silence. Finally, we hear Don walking in, saying, "What's going on?"

The lights turn on, and we stand up to sing. While

we're singing, I can't help but still feel a little weird, like I shouldn't be allowed to sing. I wouldn't be an alien if I were still living in Mexico. I'd be natural there.

As soon as the music ends, Don says, "Thank you. This means so much. I left the Philippines for a better life in the United States. I'm honored to be an American."

Don looks happy. He is even crying a little bit. I guess it's because he is no longer an alien.

Everyone applauds right away, except for me. It takes me a second. But I know it would be wrong if I didn't applaud, so I force myself to lift up my hands and hit them together. Although I might feel bad, I'm still happy for Don, and it's his big day. As we clap, my mind wonders, *If I become a citizen, will I finally feel normal? Will I be as happy as Don looks?* That makes me feel a little hopeful. The cake that Ms. Bell promised after the ceremony also helps.

Chapter Six

Once a week, I leave my regular class for speech class. Speech is where I learn to speak *properly*. This means how all the letters and words are supposed to sound in English. At least that's what my speech teacher, Ms. Thompson, says.

"Good morning, Stella!" Ms. Thompson says as I enter the room. Ms. Thompson is seated at the center of a bean-shaped table in a small room. As usual, she is dressed like a ballet teacher, in a black turtleneck and with her red hair pulled back in a bun.

"Good morning, Ms. Thompson," I say as I hesitantly sit down across from her.

"How is your dad doing?"

"Good," I say, looking down while tapping my fingers on the table.

When I first started seeing Ms. Thompson, she would come over to our apartment for after-school lessons. This was when I was in kindergarten. Dad would be home during the lessons because Mom worked. Ms. Thompson got along really well with Dad. He is very likable. He can always make people laugh, even if they can't quite understand what he says all the time. Dad speaks English worse than I do. He even talked to Ms. Thompson about taking speech classes to improve his pronunciation, but it never happened.

Back then, my parents had just divorced and Dad still lived in Chicago. He had a job, but it was only part-time at a karaoke store that his friend owned. When I asked him what he did there, he said that he kept inventory of the machines they sold. I don't know what that means, but I do know that when *absolutely* no one else was in the store, I'd sing while he stared at the computer. He didn't work there long though. Dad has never been good at keeping jobs. He lived in his own tiny apartment then. It was the size of my room with a kitchen!

"Is he still in Colorado?"

"Yes," I say, grabbing my cheeks with my hands. They feel warm.

A couple of years ago, Dad's brother, my Tío Carlos, gave Dad a job at his store in Colorado. Now Dad lives in his own house and goes skiing almost every day in winter. I know because he shows me pictures he takes with his professional camera.

"Is your dad visiting for the holidays?" she asks.

I shake my head no.

"Too bad. It would be good for you to be together," she says.

I sigh. I can never tell her what I really think, like that I don't want my parents to get back together, or that I don't really miss my dad. It would sound mean.

But why should I? All they did was argue about secret "grown-up things." What the "grown-up things" were about I don't know, but I do know it made Mom sad, which is not good at all. Nick tells me he'll explain to me when I'm older.

And I don't really miss Dad because he never keeps his promises. When he still lived in Chicago, he promised to teach me how to ride a bike, but he never did. He'd also forget to pick up Nick and me from school half the time, especially when he got a girlfriend. Walking home in the snow with a heavy backpack is never fun. Now when it comes to my birthday, I just get free things from my uncle's store. If I ask my dad for anything, even a book, it never comes.

"*Sí,*" I say, hoping a short answer will make the conversation end. I just wish she would stop asking so many questions.

"No Spanish right now, Stella." She always says that when I accidentally say a word in Spanish.

"It's not like I even speak that much anyway . . ." I mutter.

"What's that, Stella? Make sure to enunciate." She lifts up her hand to her mouth.

"Nothing," I say. I hope that was clear enough.

Just then the other students, Janelle and Roman, walk into the room. Finally, a break for me. I scribble swirls on my notebook page as she asks them how they are doing. Roman talks for a while. He is all excited that his family is going back home to Russia for the holidays. Roman is always jazzed to talk since he just graduated from ESL classes to regular classes.

We begin today's session like we normally do, with mouth exercises. We puff up our cheeks like puffer fish and follow that with deep breathing. That's to make sure we are speaking from our stomachs.

Then we practice our "th" and "busy bees" over and over. Since day one, Ms. Thompson has been correcting my pronunciations using a bag full of flash

cards that have pictures of clowns, bees, and other things. I remember it took a really long time for her to agree that I was saying "three" and "tree" differently.

From there we go through the alphabet, which isn't too bad even though there are a couple of letters, like the vowels, that sound different in Spanish.

"For good measure," she says.

I do well except for V and B. It's been three years and she still doesn't like how I say V and B.

Despite how annoying it can be, speech class can also be a little escape. I get to leave my class and be in a small, quiet room with just two other kids. It's especially good now, since I keep turning *roja* around Stanley. The other day, he asked me what time it was. I was so surprised I spilled my bucket of colored pencils on the floor.

After the alphabet, we practice big words.

"Stella, can you say 'refrigerator'?" Ms. Thompson asks.

I nod and stare at her as I say, "Refrigerator."

"Good, Stella! Maybe just a little louder next time?"

I groan. People are always telling me to speak up. I can never really figure out why. It sounds loud in my head.

"Janelle, can you say 'refrigerator'?"

Janelle says a word I don't recognize.

At least I sound better than her, I think. Then I feel a little bad. Janelle gets made fun of by some of the kids at school. She has a lisp, which makes everything she says hard to understand. She always sounds like she's eating a peanut butter sandwich. Despite everything, Janelle is still really friendly and kind. I

always try to be extra nice to her in speech and wave to her at recess.

I look up at the clock. Only thirty minutes left. Good. I'm really excited to get back to class today. We are going to play math games to see who can add, subtract, and multiply the fastest. I am really good at it, and it's the only time I like Ms. Bell calling me in front of the class.

I love showing people that I'm smart whenever I can. Numbers are also easy to say, not like letters. Whenever I hear someone spell a word out loud, my brain goes weird. It slows down like the gears on a rusty bike. I worry people think I look stupid, which I hate.

After we practice other big words like "conditioner" and "computer," Ms. Thompson sends us back to class. "Before you go, here is a treat for working so hard."

Ms. Thompson gives us stickers when we do a good job, and they are excellent stickers. Sometimes, if we do really well, she even has the ones that you can scratch and sniff. I have a binder filled with them at home. When I look at or think of my binder, I feel a little better about Ms. Thompson. Each sticker shows how much I've improved my speech all because of her.

I get two scratch-and-sniff stickers today: a strawberry one and a grape one for my collection.

"Thank you, Ms. Thompson," I say, looking her in the eyes.

"You're welcome, my dear," she says, looking back.

I smell my stickers as I leave the room.

I race back from speech and find Ms. Bell standing in front of the class. Everyone is in a new seat. She mixes us around when we're playing math games so we can go against new students.

"Perfect timing, Stella! We're about to start." She points to an empty chair.

"Why don't you take a seat at the table with Jessica Anderson and Ben Shaw?"

I walk over to the table and try to sit down, but Jessica won't move over. I clear my throat, hoping she'll take the hint. I want to say something to Jessica, but I'm afraid she'll say something mean. Ben finally moves over to make space for me. I like Ben. He's so easygoing. He just likes making everyone laugh.

Ms. Bell looks at Stanley and says, "Now, Stanley, this is your first time. So just try to do your best. Everyone else, you know the drill."

Stanley says, "Yes, ma'am."

Ms. Bell laughs. "What good manners you have, Stanley."

There's a gold whistle around Ms. Bell's neck that she blows to start each round. At the beginning of each round, she turns over a card with a math problem. Ms. Bell says we're playing spelling-bee style. I'll have to take her word for it since I've never done a spelling bee before. Whoever gets the answer right goes to the next round until there are only two players left. The questions start really easy, like two plus two equals four, but they get way harder toward the end.

"Ready?" Ms. Bell blows the whistle.

A few kids get knocked out right away, but I get all the answers correct. I feel proud that everyone can see that I'm smart. Before I know it, I'm at the last round, and it's me, Michelle, and Stanley. I'm stunned. Michelle is always good at math, but Stanley? I didn't expect Stanley to be this good at math. As Michelle sits down, I start to feel a little nervous. It's now Stanley Mason with me in the last round. Everyone is cheering for Stanley.

"Go, Stanley!" Jessica says.

Ms. Bell grabs the last flash card and asks us if we're ready. I nod my head yes. "Focus," I say to myself. Stanley grins at me and says, "I'm ready!"

I feel *roja* again and turn my head to Ms. Bell. She flips the card. It's four times seven.

"Twenty-eight," I think, but I can't talk. I'm trying so hard to get the words out, but my mouth is too dry. I even try puffing up my cheeks like we do in speech class, but nothing is working! My mouth only feels drier.

Then I hear Stanley pipe up. "Twenty-eight!"

Ms. Bell says, "Correct! You're the winner, Stanley!"

"Way to go, Stanley!" the class cheers.

I just cover my *roja* face with my hands. This is a new low. I couldn't even say numbers today.

Chapter Seven

Nick has started basketball practice in the mornings, so Mom drops me off at school now. I miss walking with Nick, but I love riding in the car with Mom. She always plays salsa music. We even dance in the car a little bit before school.

"*¡Que tengas un bien día!*" she says, passing me my backpack and kissing me on the cheek.

"And you have the greatest

day, too!" I reply. She hugs me super tight before I hop out of the car.

As I enter the school, I can still smell Mom's perfume, which makes me feel cozy and safe. It's almost like *I'm* wearing her fresh laundry and lavender scent, like a sophisticated grown-up. Then I notice Stanley out of the corner of my eye. Immediately, I start feeling *roja*. I begin to power walk toward the front door, but Stanley apparently is also a fast walker. So I do the only thing I can think of—I run into the school office.

"Do you need anything, Stella?" asks Ms. Green with a raised eyebrow. She's standing behind the front desk.

"Nothing. Just wanted to say hi." I smile while peeking out the window of the office.

"Oh, how sweet. Good morning," she replies. She reaches into a jar. "Here, take a lollipop, Stella."

"Thanks!" I say, grabbing a cherry lollipop from her hands.

I check the window again. The coast is clear, so I

say goodbye. Thankfully, we start with sustained reading in class. This means I can hide from Stanley and everyone else with a book in front of my face. I'm more mortified than usual. I'm used to the rest of the class thinking I'm odd, but from the way I've been acting, Stanley must think I'm the weirdest klutz ever.

I take a small break from fishes to read another biography about Jacques Cousteau. As interesting as Mr. Cousteau is, and, trust me, he is (he invented the Aqua-Lung, the portable breathing device that scuba divers use!), I keep thinking about Stanley. Only a little bit. I just don't know what to say to someone who is the best at everything! He's a fast runner. He can balance a spoon on his nose at lunch. He can play the drums in music class. He's new and has already made so many friends. I've been here forever, and I only have Jenny, and she's not even in my class. It's almost as if he has superpowers, magic, or is just really lucky. Whatever it is, I wish I could steal some, then everything would just be so much easier.

Fortunately, I don't have time to think too much, because after sustained reading we head to gym class with Coach Smith, who announces that we will be playing kickball.

"Boys versus girls," he says with his loud voice. His big voice matches his size. Coach Smith is the tallest person I know. In kindergarten, all I could see was his freckly knees when I was sitting crisscross-applesauce-style on the ground.

"Chop! Chop!" he says, clapping his giant hands.

The class divides up, with the boys on one side and the girls on the other. The girls decide that

Michelle should be the team captain. Everyone knows that she'd be the best since she plays sports outside of school. Then we decide what order to go in.

Michelle says, "Stella's really good at running. She should go first."

It's true. Every gym class, we get to run laps around the gym. Coach Smith always puts on fun music to run to. When Jenny and I were in the same class, we used to sing along, which slowed us down. Now that Jenny's in a different class, I just run quietly. Turns out, I can run faster than most of the girls and a couple of the boys.

I nod and smile at Michelle.

I find that if I at least smile, people think that I'm nice and I don't really have to talk. As the game starts, I am excited to get up to the plate, but then I see Stanley. He's the pitcher for the boys' team. I freeze and miss the ball when Stanley throws it at me.

The girls groan. Michelle yells, "Just kick, Stella!"

Then Jessica Anderson shouts, "Stella stares. Stella stares!"

Everyone else starts saying it, too. After three misses, I sit down on the grass by myself. I wish I could find the magic words to say to make everyone stop.

When we get back to class, I stay by myself and rest my head on my desk. It's almost lunchtime. At least that will be a break from this tough day.

"Class, before you go to lunch," Ms. Bell says, standing up, "I want to introduce a new ongoing project. It's on animals. You can choose any animal or favorite type of animal you want to research. Make sure it's an animal you really enjoy because we'll be working on this until the spring."

I lift my head. I know exactly what I'm going to do!

"We can talk about it more after lunch, but here is a handout for now," she says. As she walks around to pass out a handout with details, everyone starts talking about ideas for their projects.

"I'm going to do bears," says Ben. "You know, because of the circus bears!"

"I'm doing birds," says Lauren, who smiles at me. Lauren is quiet like me. Sometimes we talk about Nancy Drew books.

Jessica Anderson asks, "What are you going to do, Stella?" Her ponytail is swinging from side to side.

I nervously reply, "Fishes . . ."

"Makes sense," she whispers. "Fish don't talk. They just stare."

I groan and cover my face. Could this day get any worse?

I'm so happy to see Jenny at lunch. I'm also glad to see that she's alone and not with Anna. Thank goodness, too, because I need my best friend, especially on a day like today. We each bring our lunch, so we sit together right away.

I tell her what happened during kickball.

"Jessica Anderson said I never speak and that I just stare and then everyone started saying it."

"You talk plenty around me," Jenny says as she takes a bite of her Vietnamese sandwich. Vietnamese sandwiches are very yummy. They are made on soft French rolls with vegetables, tofu or meat, and mayo. Jenny brings me one sometimes for lunch.

"I know!" I say, offering her a jicama stick. Jicama is sort of like potato and watermelon mixed together, and it isn't very sweet. We squeeze a bit of *limón* on it and this sweet-spicy powder called *picosito*.

Jenny grabs one and takes the world's smallest bite. Jenny likes seeing how many bites she can make in one carrot stick and other types of food. She's up to thirty-seven in one carrot and fifty-two bites in a pretzel.

"Maybe we can write a whole list of things you can say," Jenny suggests after she takes another tiny bite of the jicama stick.

"Like 'I'm glad the sun is out,'" I say. "Or 'That is a nice outfit.' My mom says everyone likes a compliment."

"Totally! We can work on it on the playground during our recess. I've got my trusty journal," Jenny says.

Jenny's journal has a big white tiger with sparkles on the cover. If she were still in my class, she would have done her animal project on tigers. Instead, her class is doing different countries for their long project. Of course, Jenny chose Vietnam. Jenny went to Vietnam last summer for a family reunion. She brought me back chopsticks and slippers. I promised her next time I went to Mexico, I'd bring her something special like an *alebrije*, which is a little sculpture of an imaginary animal. *Alebrijes* are simply beautiful, with all different patterns and colors.

During recess, we make a whole list of things I can say until we get bored.

I slump over as I look at the list. "Jenny, I don't know if this will help . . ."

"It might." Jenny stands up and brings her fingers to her forehead. She has an idea. She lifts her arms into the air, spreads her fingers wide, and says, "I know! You can use the power of deduction!"

"Deduct ... what?" I can't even say the word; there are too many letters.

"Deduction. It's something Sherlock Holmes says. Anyway it's just asking questions. People love questions! You can ask them about their day or what they are doing. Then you'll know more about them, which means it will be easier to talk to them. It's like your own personal game of twenty questions!"

"Maybe." Sounds easier said than done.

She grabs my hand. "Come on. Let's go to the swings!"

We sit in the swings and go as high as we can. Afterward, Jenny hangs upside down from the jungle gym while I just sit on top of it. Jenny is really brave and can do flips. I am always too scared that I'll fall. She always looks so funny with her super-straight black hair hanging upside down.

"Come on, let's practice. Ask me questions," says Jenny as she pulls herself right side up again.

I draw a blank, so I ask an easy one.

"Do you like dogs or cats?"

"Stella, you know it's cats! Ask me harder ones," she says, lowering herself off the monkey bars.

Presto! I have a good one. "Who is Sherlock Holmes?"

"Excellent one, Stella!" she says, jumping onto the balance bars.

Jenny then starts telling me all about Sherlock Holmes: how he is a famous detective from a series of books, and how she recently watched part of the Sherlock Holmes movie at her cousin's house. From there, it's so easy coming up with more questions to ask Jenny, like about her cousins and what they do to-gether. But then again, it's always easy to talk to Jenny.

Even though I'm get-
ting the hang of it, it's
no mystery that what I
really need is Jenny in
my class.

Chapter Eight

A week before Thanksgiving, Mom comes home from work in a great mood.

"*Niños*, want to go to Fantastic Time Machine?"

Our favorite restaurant is Fantastic Time Machine, but we usually only go for special occasions.

"Is it somebody's birthday?" asks Nick.

"No, just a good day at work. It can be our *un*-birthday party though, if you want." Mom raises her eyebrows up and down.

I jump and clap while Nick just shrugs his shoulders yes.

"Can I invite Jenny?" I ask.

She gives me the thumbs-up and says, "And, Nick, you can invite Jason if you want."

I like Jason. He is the nicest of all of my brother's friends. They usually talk about comics and go for bike rides.

I hug Mom around the waist and ask, "Can Jenny sleep over, too?"

"Of course!"

I run to my room to call Jenny. It's going to be the best unbirthday ever.

We leave to pick up Jenny and Jason on the way to Fantastic Time Machine and stop at Jenny's first. Her mom answers the door, dressed in a uniform. Jenny's mom is about to go work the night shift at a computer company. She also does beauty treatments in a salon during the day, when she's not too tired. Ms. Le is strong like my mom. She takes care of Jenny all by herself, too.

"Hi, Stella," says Jenny's mom.

"Hi, Ms. Le!"

"I'm almost ready!" I hear Jenny yelling from the other room.

Jenny told me once that when her parents first divorced, she had to share a bed with her mom. That's when she was living in a much smaller apartment. Jenny never let me see that place. I think she was embarrassed. I've never met her dad either, and Jenny never talks about him. Jenny has met my dad though. He took us to sushi last year. Thanks to Jenny, I already knew how to use chopsticks. The sushi was tasty except for the wasabi, which I thought was avocado. I put the whole thing in my mouth while Dad was talking to the waitress. That was a bad idea. It turns out wasabi is not avocado at all and is very spicy. I had to drink a whole glass of water and eat a bowl of rice before my eyes stopped watering. Not to mention I had a runny nose the rest of the night. The sushi was also really expensive, more than Mom ever spends on dinner. I'm not really sure why. It looks like they didn't really have to cook it.

"Okay, ready!" Jenny shouts, running to the front door.

Jenny's mom speaks Vietnamese to Jenny, and Jenny disappears again. I can't understand anything they are saying to each other. I wonder if that is how it sounds when I speak Spanish with Mom in front of Jenny.

Jenny reappears with a plate covered with foil.

"Here, eggrolls," says Ms. Le.

I beam. I'm the only friend who gets eggrolls to take home from Jenny's mom.

"Thanks, Ms. Le. They are always so delicious."

She pats my shoulder. "Bye, Stella."

I happily carry the eggrolls as we walk back to the car.

Now Fantastic Time Machine looks like nothing from the outside, but it is amazing in the inside. There is red velvet everywhere with neon signs. Even the salad bar is neat because it's inside a red 1950s car. The coolest part is that all the waiters dress up in costumes as famous people and characters. They definitely stand out, while all the customers sort of blend in. In our section there is an Elvis, at

least two different Batmans, a Cinderella, and many more. My personal favorite is Einstein. The guy playing Einstein is young, but he's wearing a crazy white wig and a mustache and has beakers attached to his lab coat.

"Do you know what E equals?" he asks me.

"MC squared," I say.

"Indeed. E also equals Excellent."

Jenny whispers, "You should be talking to Cinderella. She's glamorous."

I roll my eyes. Jenny likes everything that is girly.

Nick and Jason like talking to the Batmans. They argue over which Batman is better. Even Mom talks to Elvis for a little bit.

I order spaghetti and meatballs. It's good, but not as good as Mom's e-spaghetti. It's probably because they don't know about adding the extra *sabor* like Mom does. It doesn't matter though, because we're having too much fun. After dinner we go dancing upstairs. I typically don't like dancing away from home, but it's dark with really fun lights so it's easy to blend in.

There are a bunch of kids dancing, too. I don't know any of them, so I don't care. We all drink Shirley Temples, which sounds like a grown-up drink. It's just pink soda with a cherry. In our group it's mostly Mom, Jenny, and me dancing, although I do get Nick to dance with me for a second. After a little while, Mom starts to look tired and says, "Whew! Long day at work. Keep dancing, girls! I'll check in on the boys."

She sits down next to Jason and Nick, who are playing arcade games.

When Jenny and I are alone, we get pretty silly. Jenny and I start to make up crazy dance moves.

"I'm doing the Monkey!" says Jenny while swinging her arms around.

"I'm doing the Shark!" I say, then put my hands together over my head.

"I'm doing the Chicken!" says Jenny, flapping her arms.

"I'm doing the Stingray!" I say, then spread my arms out.

We giggle. We keep dancing until I hear, "Hey, look, it's Stella Stares."

It's Jessica. Next to her is her friend Bridget, who is in Jenny's class.

I stop dancing and Jessica giggles. "Nice moves."

Bridget adds, "For someone who can't talk."

I turn *roja* while Jenny pulls me away. "Come on, Stella. It's gotten super boring here."

Jessica shouts, "Good thing you've got your translator."

I'm slouching as Jenny and I leave the dance floor. I can still hear Jessica and Bridget laughing.

We walk over to Mom. Nick is explaining to her the new comic he is reading while playing a race-car game with Jason.

Mom looks up at me. "Everything okay, Stella?" she asks, concerned.

"Yup. Just tired."

I pretend to yawn, stretching my arms way above my head. Sometimes I can be a pretty good actress.

"*No problema.* After Nick finishes his game, *nos vamos!*" She grabs her car keys out of her purse.

As we're leaving, Jenny whispers, "Why didn't you tell your mom?"

I shrug, pretending that it didn't really bother me. "We were all having fun, right?" I say, lying through my teeth.

I hate it when the kids make fun of me, but I don't want Mom to know. It's sort of embarrassing, and I don't want her to worry. Mom already spent all this money to take us to Fantastic Time Machine. I don't want to ruin her night.

When we get home, I persuade Nick to set up the tent in the backyard. He agrees only because Jason says he will help. That and it's not too cold outside.

Nick and I have set it up once before, when we pretended we were mountain people in our backyard. We only ate jerky and berries because I remembered reading that in the *Little House in the Big Woods* book.

This time

it's very different. Jenny decides that we should try to make it even more like a house, so we bring out the air mattress and pillows. Jenny wants to bring Pancho, too, but I don't want him to get cold. He's a tropical fish, after all.

"This is much better than regular camping," she says.

"Best of all, we can run into the house to use the bathroom," I say.

"And grab more nail polish."

I nod my head. I'm not good at painting my nails, but Jenny likes doing it and always makes our nails look pretty. I need to practice because I'd like to be able to paint little cat and fish designs for us.

Jenny falls asleep before I do. I lie awake wishing I didn't have to go back to school on Monday. Then I come up with a better wish. I wish for a real Fantastic Time Machine so that I could time travel. I'd travel back to earlier this night and tell Jessica off. First, I just have to come up with the perfect comeback. I think and think, but nothing comes to mind. Maybe

I *do* just stare, and maybe I *do* need Jenny to talk for me. So I decide I'd still travel back to earlier tonight, except I'd tell Jessica's parents to stay home instead of going out. That would work, too.

Chapter Nine

This year, my relatives from Mexico City come to visit for Thanksgiving. Even though we don't even celebrate Thanksgiving in Mexico, my family still likes to visit then. Actually, I kind of think they are obsessed with it. Mom uses all the recipes from *Betty Crocker*, the most American cookbook, for our Thanksgiving meal, and my relatives get excited about it. American food is exotic to them!

Still, our dinner is not just American food. Mom makes a couple of special Latin dishes like *picadillo* and *elote*. She also likes to have some of my relatives' favorite foods as snacks when they're here, like guava, *pan tostado,* and papaya.

To buy the special foods, we have to go to another town. It's very different from where we live—almost all the signs are in Spanish. It's a little far, so the only times we go are when we need to go to a store called *La Sorpresa*.

"Let's go pick up some supplies! Things for your *tía* and *abuelo*," Mom says as she drives to our favorite store.

La Sorpresa means "surprise" in Spanish. It's sort of the perfect name for the store. Even though it's small, it's filled with so many shelves that every turn is like a surprise.

The biggest surprises happen when we get to the produce area. I see so many interesting vegetables and fruits. There are prickly pears, coconuts, yuca, and huge bananas called plantains that are not really bananas. I even see cactus!

"People eat this?" I ask my mom, poking at one of the cactus leaves.

"*Sí*, it's *nopales*. You like it."

I gulp. This is *nopales*? "You mean I've been

eating cactus?" I don't understand why I haven't noticed the spiny needles going down my throat.

She laughs, knowing what I'm thinking. "You take off the needles before you cook it, that's why."

"Whew . . ."

Nick grabs a piece of a wrapped golden cake that looks like pound cake except it has sesame seeds. "Wait, this is a *quesadilla*, Mom?"

"Oh, that's delicious. Grab some. They eat that in El Salvador. Your grandmother makes it sometimes."

Mom's mom, my *abuela*, loves to cook. Because Abuela grew up in El Salvador, she makes all these different dishes from Central America, Cuba, and Spain. She even makes Italian because some members of her family were from Italy. Boy, I'm happy about that, too. Mom knows how to make lots of those delicious dishes because of Abuela.

"I thought *quesadillas* were with tortillas and cheese?" says Nick.

"They are, but that's a Mexican *quesadilla*. This is a Salvadoran *quesadilla*."

I get quiet as soon as I start thinking about all the countries that speak Spanish. There are so many and all of them are different in their own ways: they have different foods and even different ways of speaking Spanish. I barely know anything about them, especially Mexico, where I am from. Then I realize that as much as I think I might fit in better in Mexico than in the United States, I really wouldn't. I know only a handful of things about Mexico from my family, definitely not enough to make me feel like I fit in.

The truth is, we don't go back to Mexico City too often because it's very expensive to get there. I do know that Mexico City used to be the world's largest city. When I close my eyes and picture it in my head, it makes Chicago seem small. Mom used to say that when Nick first got to Chicago, he would say everything was flat and empty. He later changed his mind after we drove through Iowa.

"Mom, tell me about Mexico City again," I ask, wanting to picture where we came from.

"Mexico City is in a valley surrounded by two volcanoes. One volcano is called Popocatépetl. The other is Iztaccíhuatl. According to Aztecs, Iztaccíhuatl is a princess and Popocatépetl is the warrior who protects her."

She's told me about the volcanoes a bunch of times, but I still love hearing about them. It makes me feel like I come from a place that's special, and that I'm connected to that place through her. Mom continues telling us about her home as we stroll through the aisles of the grocery store. I see other families and smile at them. They smile back. I wish I felt more comfortable speaking with them. Still, hearing so much Spanish feels nice to my ears. It's like a warm blanket. Plus, there are so many fun words that sound better in Spanish than in English. Like *café* instead of "coffee" or *buenísimo* instead of "really good." Although I would never use both words in the same sentence. *Café* is not *buenísimo*. It's gross.

Nick pushes the cart while Mom grabs glass jars of pimentos and *aceitunas* off the shelves. If they weren't too hard to open, I'd eat the *aceitunas* right away. I love olives almost as much as I love *albóndigas*. Next, Mom searches for the guava and the cheese. Then she checks things off the list and scans down, pausing after a second.

"Your *abuelo* likes *matrimonios* when we play cards." Mom's face lights up as she says *abuelo*.

Mom is very close to her dad. When my parents divorced, he stayed with us for a month. He even walked me to school every day. He is also the only person I try to speak Spanish with other than Mom. That's because he lets me talk really, really slowly and takes the time to listen to me. He's so nice that I don't even mind when he laughs at me for saying the words wrong or not rolling my r's.

Mom reviews her list one last time. "We almost forgot the *frijoles*," she says, pushing the cart back toward the aisle with the canned beans. As Mom searches for the *frijoles*, I see a girl my age talking to her *abuelo* in Spanish. For a moment, I feel a little jealous. My jealousy is quickly replaced with a sinking feeling in my stomach. I realize that my relatives are going to be here tomorrow. I cross my fingers and hope that I'll wake up knowing more Spanish.

Chapter Ten

The next day, Nick and I wait at home while Mom picks up my relatives at the airport. She doesn't take us because she says we'll get bored at the airport. Because my relatives are coming in from a different country, they have to go through customs, which is where they check you to make sure you are not bringing any illegal goods into the country. It can take a really long time.

This trip it's only Mom's sister, my Tía Juanis, and my Abuelo Apolinar. I haven't seen them in two years, so I'm a little nervous. Abuela rarely comes because she's very particular and doesn't like traveling anymore. She'd rather just stay at home playing cards. It would be easier if it were my Tía Margarita visiting. She comes more often because she travels the world all the time and sometimes stays over in Chicago for a day or two in between her trips. Of all my relatives, she speaks English the best, so I like talking to her the most. She also is very creative, a professor, and speaks four languages. I want to be as smart as her when I grow up.

While she's gone, Mom puts Nick in charge of watching the turkey. My job is to set the table. I know that's because I have an artistic eye. Nick doesn't know how to fold the napkins into triangles like they do in the fancy restaurants on TV. I even make little name tags in the shape of a turkey for everyone's seat. For a while, the house is quiet and I'm able to draw. Part of me wants to hide

in bed with a book instead of doing Thanksgiving. I feel anxious, almost like it is the first day of school again.

But before I can go hide, I hear the front door.

"*¡Hola, mi amor!*" says Juanis in a loud voice. She swallows me up in a big hug and kisses both my cheeks. I can't see anything because of her fuzzy sweater, but I can smell her perfume. Juanis wears a lot of makeup. That's different from Mom, who only wears a little makeup when she goes to work.

Juanis pulls away from me, then goes to Nick. I can finally see that she's wearing a crazy patterned sweater and leggings. Her short red hair looks wilder than I have ever seen it.

"*Hola. ¡Que guapo!*" she says as Nick beams. He likes being called good-looking.

Juanis gets along really well with Nick. She used to take care of him after school when we lived in Mexico City. I sit on the couch and draw while Nick talks to Juanis in Spanish.

I don't get a chance to talk to my family as much. To them, I am just the *artista* who makes drawings.

They don't really know me like they know Nick. He was in first grade when we left, while I was just a baby. They don't know what questions to ask me, like what is my favorite fish or my favorite book. And even if they did, I wouldn't know how to tell them in Spanish. So I let them talk without me.

Abuelo walks in next with Mom. He's a little slow because he has a limp from losing one of his legs in a bus accident when he was my age. He manages to get around everywhere thanks to his wooden leg, but he never complains about it. Even when he takes his wooden leg off at night, he whistles as he hops into bed.

"*Hola, que preciosa está Stella,*" Abuelo says. When he calls me pretty, I have to admit I feel a little less weird. He puts down his guitar and laughs a big belly laugh as he hugs me with both arms.

Abuelo sniffs the air. "*¿Dónde está la comida, Nick?*" Abuelo is obviously hungry as he hugs Nick.

"*Casi,*" says Mom, which means the food is almost

ready. She takes Abuelo's bag and guitar to Nick's room. Abuelo always brings his guitar when he visits. He used to be a performer in Mexico, playing on a radio program.

We freshen up real quick, and I also feed Pancho. "Happy Thanksgiving!" I say as I drop an extra food pellet.

Then Mom says, *"¡Está listo!"* announcing that the food is ready.

Everyone sits down at the table as Mom brings out the dishes. There's turkey, cornbread stuffing, mashed potatoes, and roasted vegetables. We even have sweet potatoes with marshmallows! Mom says she saw the recipe in a cookbook, but I think it's weird.

My favorite things to eat are the dishes that are not American. We make this stuffing called *picadillo*, which is ground meat with *aceitunas*. The olives make it feel special, like it's our own treat. Mom also makes *elote*, corn on the cob with crumbled Mexican cheese on top.

I want to dig in, but Mom says we have to say what we are grateful for first. Everyone says a few things in Spanish. When it comes to my turn, I just say very quietly, *"Mi familia."* I feel as shy as I do when I'm at school, but this is different. At school I'm only shy about saying the words right, but here, around my family, I just don't have the words to say everything I want to say. If I could have said what I'm grateful for in English, I would easily have gone on and on. There's so much! Like all the sea creatures in the sea, Mom, Nick, and Jenny, my best friend. But I can't. Not in Spanish.

I do try sometimes. But when I try to speak Spanish, Juanis will finish my sentences for me. Like when I say,

"*Quiero . . .*" I say, looking at the *picadillo*.

"*Más pavo,*" says Juanis, who starts putting more turkey on my plate, which is not at all what I wanted.

I push my turkey around with my fork. It's hard to want to talk when people aren't even listening to you.

We eat until we are stuffed like *pavos*. Mom decides to look at photo albums before dessert. "*Vamos a mirar fotos de la familia.*"

It's funny to see pictures from before I was born. Everyone is wearing different-looking clothes, not to mention their different hairstyles. Both Mom *and* Dad had long hair! Nick had blond hair instead of the dark brown hair he has now. There are even pictures of Dad with his family and Mom's family.

Nick points to a picture. He is hitting a *piñata* with Dad, Abuelo, and my dad's brother, Carlos. "I remember that. That was when I turned four years old," he says.

"And these are the puppets I had at my birthday

party." He points to this picture with these amazing wooden puppets.

Mom, Juanis, and Abuelo nod. Nick remembers so much.

On another page, I see another picture of Abuelo, Tío Carlos, and a woman I don't know toasting.

"Mom, who is that?" I ask.

"Oh, that's your Abuela Carmen on your dad's side. Her hair is a little different there. That's probably why you didn't recognize her."

I've only seen Dad's parents once since we've moved to the United States. While the grown-ups talk, I ask Nick, "Is Tío Carlos nice?"

"He is. Or at least he was back then. He'd play *fútbol* with me and Dad."

I sort of remember seeing my *tío*. He used to live near us. We'd see him regularly until my parents divorced. Then we stopped seeing him and he moved to Colorado.

Mom flips to pictures of when I was born. These are my favorite. I like seeing the pictures of me with

tiny little bows in my hair. Everyone agrees that I was the cutest baby. There are also photos of everyone holding me, including Nick. He leans over and messes up my hair.

"*La bebé,*" Juanis says. She touches my arm and gives me a kiss on the cheek. She immediately wipes the pink lipstick off my cheek and grabs my chin.

"*Tú sabes que soy tu segunda madre, Stella,*" Juanis says. Sometimes she likes to tell me she's my second mother.

I nod my head. "*¡Sí!*"

Juanis might not always listen, but I know she loves me.

After we've given our stomachs a break, we eat three different kinds of pie: apple, pecan, and pumpkin. I show Juanis and Abuelo my drawings of the animal project while we eat.

"*¡Que bueno!*" Abuelo says they are really good. He especially likes my manatee.

Nick then begs Abuelo to play the guitar, and he begins to play many songs I know. I love singing along, but sometimes I stay quiet to watch Mom sing. She looks so happy singing with her dad.

Mom looks at me. "You know, when I was your age, your *abuelos* would have these amazing parties. Abuelo and all his musician friends would sing all night."

"But what about your bedtime?"

Mom laughs. She translates what I said to Abuelo and Juanis, and it makes them laugh, too.

"*Ayi, Stella,*" says Abuelo.

I tap Mom's arm. "Why is that funny?"

Mom sees that my eyebrows are raised up.

"Don't worry, *mi chiquita*. It was just cute. Things are a little different in Mexico. Families throw more parties and people are a little less strict with bedtimes."

"I wouldn't mind that," says Nick.

I don't say anything. Part of me wishes we never left Mexico. Sure, the parties and less strict bedtimes would be great, but I also think things would have been easier. We would see each other all the time instead of once every other year. If I lived near them, then they would feel like *my* family, and not like visitors or just like Mom's or Nick's family. Mom

also wouldn't have to do everything by herself and we wouldn't be alone anymore.

Abuelo starts singing my favorite song, *"El Corrido de Chihuahua,"* and motions to me with his guitar. I know all the words, so I start singing along.

Mom stands up. She pulls me to the floor to dance with her and twirls me until I start giggling. She finally stops twirling me, and everything keeps spinning for a second. When I can finally see straight, I notice that my whole family is giggling with me, too, even Nick. I'm really happy that giggling and smiling is something that doesn't have to be translated. You just know it when you see it.

Chapter Eleven

"Do you want to go with me to my office, Stella?" Mom asks the Sunday after Thanksgiving. "I need to catch up on some work." Mom sometimes has to go to work on the weekends when it's really busy at the office. This time it's because she took a few days off to spend time with Abuelo and Tía while they were visiting.

"Yes!" I say. I race upstairs to change out of my pajamas.

I love tagging along with Mom to work. I like to see where she spends her time every day while I'm at school. Nick normally goes biking with Jason instead, so it's our special outing.

Mom has an important job as a boss at a radio station, which means she has to look professional all the time. She even has to wear high heels that make her super tall. I like to try them on sometimes, but I can only walk in them for a second. I love the noise they make though. Since it's the weekend, we both wear sneakers instead.

Instead of driving, we ride the Metra train to Mom's work downtown. The train station is covered in signs that say "Metra: The way to really fly." As we ride the train, I like to pretend I'm a grown-up like Mom. I even borrow her briefcase to carry my fish book to read on the train. I read all about clown fish on the ride.

"Did you know the real name for a clown fish is anemonefish?"

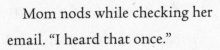

Mom nods while checking her email. "I heard that once."

"Well, did you also know that male anemonefish take care of the eggs?"

She puts down her phone. "That I did not know. Lucky anemonefish moms."

Mom looks out the window for a second. I feel bad that she has to do everything by herself. Dad's not around and he never sends money. The excuse for why he never helped before was he had no money, but now that he works for Tío Carlos there isn't really an excuse.

Mom flutters her lips and turns back toward me.

"Okay, my little sea explorer," she says, wrapping her arm around me, "tell me more fun fish facts."

After I tell her more about the anemonefish for the rest of the ride, we get to her office. I'm excited. Going to work makes me feel important and grown-up. As we enter the building, we have to wave a badge.

"What does 'closed-circuit television' mean, Mom?" I say, pointing to a sign.

"It means that there are cameras recording who comes in and out of the building."

"Cool!"

She laughs.

Near the elevator sits a security guard named Carl, who wears an official uniform. "Working again, Ms. Díaz?"

"Just for a little while, Carl."

Carl waves at me. I salute him back.

After opening a bunch of doors with Mom's badge, we finally get to where she works. From there we pass the vending machines with food I've never seen before.

"What's a honey bun, Mom?" My face is pressed up to the glass.

"I am not sure. Honestly, it's an American thing. I've never had it."

"Can I try it?" I ask, pressing my face closer.

"Maybe another time."

Mom keeps walking, and I have to run to catch up with her. Near the vending machines is a whole kitchen with a refrigerator and a bunch of tables.

"Do you eat here, Mom?"

"Sometimes. Many times, I have business lunches or I eat in my office."

As we continue to walk to her office, we pass all kinds of computer equipment. There are huge photocopy machines with so many buttons I want to push and levers I want to pull, but I don't.

Then we walk past the DJ booths, where all the people who talk on the radio work. There are even more buttons here, ones that light up, too. I recognize the voice of the DJ, but we don't really listen to this radio station too much in the car. Mom likes listening to salsa and classical music instead. That's when I notice a man in the booth. He steps out for a second and says, *"Buenos días, señora."*

"¡Hola!" she says. *"Nacho, ella es mi hija, Stella."* Mom introduces me to Nacho. I turn *roja* and hide behind Mom.

He laughs and says, *"¡Mucho gusto, Stella!"* I know that means "Nice to meet you," so to be polite I say quietly, *"Sí, igualmente."* Then I run ahead of Mom, and finally we get to her office. I love Mom's office. I usually like to lie on her couch or sit across from her desk pretending that I'm her assistant. I also like going through all her cabinets and drawers. I don't think she always likes that, but I can't help it.

"What do you want to do while I'm working, Stella?" she says as she turns her computer on. She looks a little stressed-out.

I pause, closing a drawer full of Post-it notes and pens. Then I get a great idea. "Can I write a story, Mom?"

"*¡Sí!*" she says.

While she works in her office, I decide to go to an empty cubicle. I get office supplies from the supply closet and grab every color pen they have. Then I get down to work. I decide today I'm going to write about the pirate Captain Rob and his sidekick, Monkey. Nick and I like to pretend we're pirates when we're swimming, so I dedicate it to Nick at the beginning.

I try to make it as close to a real book as possible. I put in a title page, and I even write a biography for myself at the end. When I'm done, my book is ten pages long with drawings.

I tiptoe to Mom's office. She's typing away at her computer while chewing on a pen.

"Mom?"

"*Mande*," Mom says, looking distracted.

"I finished my story."

"Wonderful. I'm almost done, too."

"Okay," I say.

But it takes her a little bit longer than she says. I get bored waiting, so I explore around the office a bit. I even make myself a cup of hot cocoa in the kitchen. That gives me even more energy, so I quietly run from cubicle to cubicle peeking in to see everyone's pictures and decorations.

Finally, I make my way back to her office.

"Sorry, Stella. Really just a couple more minutes, then we'll eat lunch," she says, typing away on the computer.

While she finishes, I lie on her couch and hang my head over the side. I look at her and her office upside down. She has a few pictures of Nick and me up on the wall. She also has one of my drawings. It's one that I did on our trip to Wisconsin Dells from a couple of years ago. It was one of our last trips as a family before my parents divorced. I did a drawing of the little deer and pine trees we saw as we rode on the sled.

I look over at Mom. Mom looks so serious as she works. I feel bad that Dad isn't so good at being a dad. If he was, Mom wouldn't have to work so hard.

I wonder if she likes her job. I don't even realize that I say it out loud.

"It's a fun job. Sometimes it's too long," she says. "And I'd rather be at home with *tú y tu hermano*. Or on the beach." She winks. "Enough work anyway. Show me your book."

I walk over to her. "Be prepared to be amazed. It's the best thing I've ever done."

"I'm sure it is."

We read my book together. It's the epic story of Captain Rob and Monkey, who go in search of treasure, and the evil pirate who tries to steal it. The story ends with a cliffhanger because I plan on writing a sequel. When we're done reading, she spins her chair to face me and gives me a hug.

"I love it, Stella. I know what will make it more official. We can do it while we're leaving."

She locks up her office, and we walk over to the room with the photocopier and the other fancy machines. She heads to the one that looks like it has giant teeth and grabs a coil, a piece of plastic, and a piece of black paper.

"*Por favor,*" she says, motioning for me to give her my story.

She puts the plastic in front. Then she puts the black paper on the back. Next, she inserts the coil around the giant teeth in the machine. Before she grabs the big handle she says, "Watch your *manitas.*"

I move my little hands. Then there is a big *snap.* My pages are bound together.

I squeal. "It's a book!"

When I go to school the next day, I walk over to Ms. Bell's desk before the class starts.

"I wrote a story over the Thanksgiving break, Ms. Bell."

"That's wonderful, Stella," Ms. Bell says. "Do you want to read it out loud to the class?"

I shake my head no.

"What if I help you, and we read only a little bit?"

"I guess so." I'm really proud of my story, and I do want to share it with the class. I just don't want to have everyone looking at me. The last thing I want is a repeat of the first day of school.

When class begins, Ms. Bell stands up in front with my book.

"Look at what one of your classmates did over the weekend. Stella drew and wrote a whole story just for fun. It's called *Captain Rob and Monkey.*"

She starts flipping through the pages. I feel *roja.*

"Cool! Pirates!" says Stanley.

Ms. Bell starts reading my story, and it actually sounds pretty good. Then she looks over to me. "Stella, would you like to read a paragraph?"

I get up. I'm shaky. I read the paragraph quickly and never look up the whole time. Then I sit back down.

"Thank you, Stella. I think you did a great job," she says as she hands me back my book. "This relates perfectly to your animal project. Class, you've all been working hard researching. Well, there is a new part to the project. You all will be presenting the projects to the class. You'll have to talk for five minutes each and show us everything you learned about your project. Now, everyone knows that just talking in front of the class can be a little boring. So I want you to make the presentations fun and exciting!"

"Like costumes?" asks Ben.

"Yes, you can wear costumes. You can do a dance. Anything is possible!"

"I'm going to wear my equestrian outfit," says

Jessica. Her family owns a horse, so naturally she's doing her project on horses.

As the whole class starts talking, I get extra quiet. Now I have to do a whole presentation with complete sentences? And it's supposed to be entertaining? Maybe if I wear a giant sheet on my head it will be less scary. Then I look down at my book. Maybe it won't be so bad. I made it through reading a paragraph in front of the whole class and didn't stumble at all! That's way better than the first day. Maybe I can do this.

I see Stanley looking at me. Then I see Jessica, who looks carefree and even excited about the presentation. Nope, I have a feeling this story isn't going to end well.

Chapter Twelve

Winters are very cold in Chicago.
Sometimes, it's hard to even want to leave the house!
It was so cold on Christmas that we just stayed
home. Plus, Mom had to work some on Christmas
Eve. Luckily, New Year's Day isn't too cold. Mom

decided we should do something special and celebrate it in Wisconsin Dells. Even though we have trees near our house, I never see as many trees as when we're in Wisconsin. The woods are so pretty. And there are so many winter activities! More than we could ever do in Chicago.

Also, I am very happy to get away. I don't want to think about the presentation or school.

"Don't you want to go to Jamaica instead?" I suggest to Mom. Jamaica is much farther away, I think.

Mom just laughs. "I wish," she says. "How about when you become a famous explorer or artist, we'll go?"

As I imagine deep-sea diving or, better yet, my artwork on display in a museum, I feel okay about not going to Jamaica quite yet.

Our favorite activity in Wisconsin Dells is snowshoeing,

so we go the moment we arrive. First, you have to wear these shoes that look like gigantic tennis rackets. They help you trek across the snow and also make you look sort of funny when you are walking.

"We look like penguins!" Mom says as we waddle in our snowshoes.

"I think we look like humpback whales because we are puffy from our clothes!" I say.

"No, we look like spies!" says Nick.

"Except if this were a spy movie, we would wear all white and we'd be running away from the bad guys who wear all black," I say.

Mom shakes her head. "If you were wearing all white, I couldn't see you. I want to be able to see my *niños*."

Because snowshoes are heavy, Mom and Nick are able to walk much faster than I can. After a while, I fall behind.

"Hey, slow down!" I say, panting.

"Sorry, slowpoke," Nick calls back.

I groan. He turns around to look at me. "You

better walk faster, too. Everyone knows that Bigfoot lives here. He especially likes to eat little girls."

"You're lying. He's not real." I stomp my foot. Then I take a quick glance around. It's eerily quiet.

"Come on, let's go. Walk a little faster, Stella. There's so much to do today!" Mom says.

Nick likes to scare me sometimes. He told me once when we were going swimming that there were alligators in the lake. It scared me so much I couldn't go in the water for the rest of the day. When we got home, I researched alligators. Turns out there are no alligators in Illinois. When I showed Nick the website, he just shrugged and said, "You never know."

Now, I am pretty sure that Bigfoot isn't real, but I can hear branches moving. It's probably just the wind, but I'm going to double-check when I get home.

I yell, "Mom!" and run to catch up with them.

I keep up, but after a while, I start feeling tired. Looking out for Bigfoot *and* wearing snowshoes is exhausting. "Nick, can you carry me?"

He squats down, and I jump on his back. "I'm only doing this because we look bigger and more intimidating to Bigfoot," he says. I can't see his face, but I know his secret smirk is there.

I giggle and hug his neck a little tighter. It's hard to stay mad at Nick for too long.

"Stella, we're almost to the car," Mom says, patting Nick's head. "We'll grab lunch, and then we'll have more fun."

During the car ride, I notice some little huts on the lake. These are for the ice fishers. Seeing them reminds me of my school project about ocean life. I haven't told Mom or Nick about the new presentation part of the project. I don't want them to think I can't do it or handle it. I think Nick would make fun of me and Mom has enough problems with work. I don't want to make her worry when she doesn't have to.

"Are you thinking about your project?" Mom asks. She can magically tell what I'm thinking without me telling her.

"Yup," I say quietly. "Mom . . ."

"Yes, Stella?"

"Do you ever get nervous talking in front of large crowds?"

"No, why?" she replies.

I sigh. That's not what I was hoping to hear. "Just curious. Really, *never*?"

She pauses. "Not really. Your *abuelo* was a performer. I was just used to seeing that."

Her response doesn't make me feel better. In fact, I feel a little worse. Thankfully, Nick says, "Oh good. There's the restaurant!"

After a hot lunch, we walk around downtown Dells. Even though it's New Year's, the streets are still covered in Christmas decorations of snowflakes, reindeer, and snowmen. I start to wonder how we would celebrate the holidays in Mexico. I can't picture

Mexico City in snow. I am also pretty sure a snowman would just melt there.

So I ask, "Mom, what did you do for Christmas in Mexico?"

"Nothing like this. It's too warm there. We just celebrated with our family and friends. Actually, Three Kings Day is kind of a bigger deal in Mexico than Christmas for kids."

"Really? I've never heard of it," says Nick.

"It's fun. You leave your shoes out and the three wise men leave you presents overnight."

"Can we do that next year?" I ask.

Nick says, "Yeah, I want more presents!"

"Well. We live in the States. I just didn't think to do it. I wanted you guys to fit in."

I sigh. I think to myself, *But I don't fit in, Mom. I am different from the people in my class. I'm an alien.*

Suddenly, I picture Pancho swimming alone in his fish tank. He can't be around other fish, but he also can't live outside of the water. He doesn't belong anywhere either.

Chapter Thirteen

Ring. Ring.

"It's Dad!" yells Nick after he answers the phone. I run over.

"Really?" I whisper. It's January, and we just spoke to him on Christmas. He usually never calls this soon after Christmas.

Nick nods. He covers the phone.

"He's going to be in Chicago in a couple months for work. He also wants to know whether we got our Christmas presents."

Our Christmas presents this year were more

gloves and socks from Tío's store. Big surprise. Also, like usual, they look like nothing we'd ever wear and they don't fit right.

I put my ear to the phone and listen with Nick.

"Yes, we got our presents," says Nick.

"Good. Got to make sure my *niños* are warm." Then Dad says, "You know I'd do anything for you guys."

Nick rolls his eyes. Good thing we're not on video.

When school starts back up after winter break, it's so cold we actually end up using some of the new gloves and socks. Sadly, Jenny's not there. She has a cold, which means I have to eat lunch without her, and it's a little scary. I'm not really friends with anyone else, so I'm not sure where to sit.

At lunchtime, I look around the cafeteria. My options are slim. I also know that I can't eat anywhere near Jessica. I scan the room, looking from table to table, searching for a friendly face when I finally spot Lauren, who is reading another Nancy Drew book.

Yes, I think. When I walk over, Lauren makes room for me without my even asking. I nod my head. This will be good, I think. We both like being quiet. To my surprise though, Lauren is pretty chatty today. She asks, "How's your ocean life project?"

"It's good," I say. My drawings do look good. It's the presentation I'm worried about. I pause and look at Lauren. She looks so excited, like she has a secret she wants to share. So I ask her, "How is your project?"

I've been trying to ask more questions, as Jenny suggested. It's working some, especially with Lauren.

She leans in. "Well, my project is great. Don't tell anyone, but I'm going to bring in my uncle's parrot for the presentation. Ms. Bell said it was okay." She sits up a little taller.

"That's really cool."

She nods. Lauren looks so proud. I don't mean to, but I frown for a split second. I don't know how Ms. Bell could have agreed to this. It's simply not fair. A parrot can talk and sing! That's like presenting with a partner whom you know everyone will like.

What am I going to do? I can't bring Pancho. I love him, but he doesn't talk. Most people would get bored just watching him swim. Maybe I can be like the wizard in *The Wizard of Oz* and do my whole presentation from behind a curtain.

Recess is much harder than lunch without Jenny. It's too cold to be outside, so recess is in the gym. It feels lonelier there because everyone is closer together than we would be on the playground. When Jenny is not there on a warm day, I can just hide underneath a slide.

I decide to bring my notebook and pen to recess.

I am determined to figure out my presentation. So I sit on the bleachers and open the notebook to a blank page. I write "Presentation" on top in big letters. I underline it three times.

I think.

Then think.

And *think*.

Nada. Nothing.

Frustrated, I close the notebook.

As I start looking around the gym, I see Jessica playing jump rope with a few of the girls. It looks like fun, but I feel too shy to ask to play, plus I don't want to deal with Jessica.

Unfortunately, Jessica notices that I'm looking. She curls her lips. "Stella Stares is staring."

"Maybe she's stupid," says Bridget.

I bunch my fingers into little fists by my sides when I hear the word "stupid." I can feel my heart pounding like drums in my chest. I feel hot. *Roja* with anger. People can say I'm strange or different, but I am not stupid.

I stand up without thinking and say in a loud voice, *"I'm not stupid."*

Jessica's eyes get big for a second. She looks surprised, even a little nervous, but that only lasts a moment. Bridget starts laughing and Jessica joins her.

Thankfully Stanley walks over with Ben and asks them if they want to play tag.

"Do you want to play, Stella?" Stanley asks, turning to me.

"That's okay, Stanley," I say quietly as I sit back down. If he'd asked if I wanted to play hide-and-seek, I might have said yes. I'm really a good hider and today feels like a good hiding day.

When I get home, I lie on the rug in the living room. Feeling alone is very tiring. I wish I could just move back to Mexico. Then I realize I wouldn't have been able to defend myself there like I did today. I would have just replied in English to some mean kid who was speaking Spanish. At least Jessica understood me. That's it, as soon as Mom gets home, I'm

going to ask exactly how to say "I'm not stupid" in
Spanish.

Nick walks over to the computer, sits down, and
turns it on.

"Rough day at school?" he asks as he starts to
play a video game. I sit next to him.

"Nick?"

"Yup . . ." he says. He's staring at the screen, so it feels easier to talk to him.

"Did you know we're aliens?"

He gets quiet. He pauses the game and looks at me.

"You know that's not like aliens in outer space. You're not E.T."

"I know that, but it still means we're different."

"Okay, yeah, it sounds bad, but it's really not." He opens a new window on the computer and types. Then he points to the screen. It's a very official-government-looking website.

"See, here's the definition. 'Alien' is an individual who is not a U.S. citizen or U.S. national."

I bite my lip and nod.

Seeing that that didn't really help, Nick gets another idea and types something else on the keyboard. A new window pops up.

"Look, and the word 'alien' is derived from the Latin word *alienus*, which means 'stranger' or 'foreign.'"

I look at him. "That doesn't make me feel better."

"Okay, so we're aliens, but you're not a weirdo. You're my sister. *Mi hermana.*"

"But then why do kids at school say I'm weird? Today one of them even said I was stupid, which is not the truth." I cross my arms.

Nick's face looks sad. I never really told him before that kids make fun of me sometimes.

"Sis, you're not stupid. You are the coolest, smartest almost-nine-year-old I know."

"You're just saying that," I say, looking at the ground.

"No, I'm not," he says, lifting up my chin.

"Plus, so-called 'aliens,'" he says, putting air quotes around "aliens," "are some of the smartest people. Albert Einstein was an alien. He was from Germany. He's pretty smart and cool, right?"

I nod.

"Jenny's mom is an alien."

I nod again. That's true, and if she hadn't moved here, I might never have met Jenny, which would have been terrible.

"Plus, I'm an alien, and I'm the coolest, right?" he says, putting his hand on his chest.

I move my hand side to side. "So-so."

Nick laughs and continues, "Aliens are just people from different places, and different places can be awesome. Can you imagine if we were born here? If we weren't Mexican, Mom wouldn't know how to make *albóndigas*!?"

I gasp. I hadn't considered that.

"Or worse, we'd just call them 'meatballs' instead and they would be boring meatballs *sin sabor*."

That makes me feel a little better. I like it when Nick listens to me. Still, I can't help but feel scared thinking about the presentation.

"What's the frown about?" he asks.

Nick is being so understanding that I just blurt it out.

"I have to do a presentation with my fish project. I have to speak for a whole five minutes in front of the class. I'm nervous," I confess, dropping my head into my hands.

"I remember the first time I had to do that. It was scary."

I look up. I can't even picture Nick being nervous. He's so good at school presentations. Once I saw him do a debate in front of the whole school.

"I have no idea what to do . . ." I say, scratching my head.

"Well, first of all, we will practice."

I sigh.

"Yeah, I know. It sounds silly, but it helps."

Then he pauses for a good minute. "And maybe Mom can take us to the Shedd Aquarium."

The Shedd Aquarium! Nick is the smartest! We've never been, but I've always wanted to go. It's all the way in downtown Chicago. It was the largest aquarium in the world for the longest time.

I throw my arms around him.

"All right, all right," he says, hugging me back. I can see the small smirk on his face. "It'll be good. We can do some research and get some ideas for your presentation."

"Yes!" I exclaim.

"And don't worry. I'll help you, sis," he says, then nudges me. He puts two fingers above his head like antennas.

"We aliens got to stick together."

Chapter Fourteen

"Stella, sit over here!"

I hear Jenny calling me from across the cafeteria. I walk over with my tray, and as I get closer I can see Anna is there, sitting next to Jenny. My hands start to shake, which makes my chocolate pudding jiggle on the tray. I sit down next to Jenny. Anna waves hello.

"Thanks for letting me sit with you guys," says Anna. "My best friend, Isabel, is sick today. I usually eat with her." She pouts a little bit.

I quietly let out a sigh of relief. Yes! Anna has her own best friend.

"No problem. It's hard to eat lunch without your

best friend," I say, smiling as I shove a chicken tender into my mouth.

"Thanks, Stella. Can I trade you an ants on a log for a chicken tender?" Anna holds up a piece of celery with peanut butter and raisins.

"Sure," I reply. We exchange grins as we trade food. Any person who is willing to share food with me can be my friend. The more we talk, the more I can see why Jenny is friends with Anna. She has a cat, a goldfish, and is pretty funny. I can actually picture us eating lunch together again, maybe even with Isabel.

"Do you guys have your Valentine's Day cards ready for tomorrow?" asks Jenny. "I do!"

Anna nods. "I can't wait for the class party."

I tighten my lips. "Almost. I'll finish them tonight."

Usually, I would have finished them by now, but selecting Valentine's Day cards this year has been tricky. Mom makes me give valentines to all the kids in my class, even the ones I don't like. With most kids, I can give them something simple like "Happy Valentine's Day." That works for Jessica, who I *have* to give one to, but I don't know which card to choose for Stanley. "Happy Valentine's Day" would be boring. I also can't choose the "Be MY Valentine" card. No way could I do the "Will You Be Mine?" card.

When I get home from school, I finally choose "You're the Coolest" for Stanley because it's the truth. I also spend a lot of time writing out his name nicely. I hope when he reads it he'll realize that I'm normal and not weird.

Then things will get better in class. We might even be friends.

While I write everyone else's names on their envelopes, Nick watches *Jaws* on television. "I'm helping you research for your project," he says.

Some help! I have to hide behind the couch for most of the movie. Out of all the sea creatures, I'm most afraid of great white sharks. People say they don't attack humans that often, but after watching the movie, I'm not sure. Jaws, the great white shark in the movie, really seemed to like attacking people.

The next day I bring the cards for my classmates with me. There are balloons and hearts decorating the entire classroom. I spy Mom in the corner hanging up a streamer. Mom always takes a break from work to help out with parties as the classroom mom. I love her being here. She makes it a little easier, since she is so friendly and gets to know all the kids. Also, Mom is chatty enough for the two of us, so I follow her everywhere as she walks around the room.

I'm busy eating a cupcake when I see Mom talking to Stanley. I've never told her about Stanley. He just cut his hair short, and it looks super soft. Mom says to him, "I love your haircut. My son, Nick, just cut his hair like that. Do you mind if I touch your hair? It looks like a teddy bear."

Stanley just grins and says, "Yes, ma'am."

Mom pets his head. "Yup, just like a teddy bear." They both laugh and Stanley turns a little *roja*. I'm surprised. I didn't think Stanley could ever get embarrassed.

Then I hear Jessica whisper in my ear, "Are you hiding behind your *mommy*?"

I turn around, my own face *roja*. Mom turns around, too. Apparently, Jessica wasn't quiet enough. Mom stands up extra tall and says, "Yes, I'm Stella's mother. Nice to meet you."

Jessica drops her mouth open and her face goes blank. She's been caught in the act.

I beam. "Yes, this is my mom."

Unhappy that she can't say anything else to me,

Jessica huffs, puffs, and walks away. Having Mom around is the greatest!

After the Valentine's Day party, Mom drives us home. The radio starts playing my favorite song. I open my mouth to sing, but she lowers the music.

"You know, Stella, someone can only make you feel bad if you let them. It's just words." I can see her eyes looking at me in the rearview mirror. She looks worried. I hate making her worry. I hoped that she would never find out.

"It doesn't feel like it's just words. Plus, you're lucky everyone likes you."

"Not everyone likes me. I just decided I wasn't going to let it affect me as much. It'll work for you, too. I promise."

I look out the window. At the stoplight, I feel her hand reaching back to me. I grab on to it tight. It makes me feel safe.

"You're so much stronger than you realize. That's why your full name is Estrella. You're my star. You can light up the dark."

"You promise you aren't lying?" I look into her eyes in the rearview mirror. She looks right back at me and says, "Promise."

"Thanks, Mom." I don't a hundred percent believe her, but Mom never lies.

Chapter Fifteen

"Wow, Stella. That's such a great dolphin," Ms. Bell says as she looks down at my project. She leans over to me. "Can you do me a favor? We need a poster for the third-grade spelling bee tomorrow. Since you're an expert at drawing dolphins, would you be interested in doing it?"

I sit up and exclaim, "Yes!"

"Wonderful! I'll give you the poster and materials."

Ever since I shared *Captain Rob and Monkey* with Ms. Bell, she has been giving me extra projects.

She also gives me story ideas all the time. Some of them are not that great, but I love that she talks to me as if I'm a good writer.

Dolphins are also the mascot of my school. On the last day of first grade, we got to vote for a new mascot. I voted for the dolphins because back then I mixed up cute little penguins with dolphins. I was really bummed when I saw a dolphin mural instead of a penguin mural when we got back from summer vacation.

That's when I started learning all about fishes and all marine life.

"Come, Stella. Let's go to the supply closet to see what you need."

Together we select glitter, markers, and a poster board, and she puts it in a tote bag for me.

"I can't wait to see what you'll do!" she says.

As soon as I get home, I draw a dolphin jumping with big letters that spell out "Spelling Bee." I even put glitter on the waves to make it feel more magical. I'm so happy that I even show Pancho.

"Look, Pancho!" I say. He zips around his fishbowl. I am pretty sure that means he likes it.

The next morning, I proudly stare at my poster as I eat my bowl of cereal. It's so great that my poster will be on display for everyone to see. Then I start thinking about the spelling bee. I don't mind spelling out loud too much, but I also have never done a spelling bee in my life.

I ask Nick, "Have you ever done a spelling bee before?"

"Yup. They're pretty fun. Let's practice. I'll quiz you."

"Okay," I reply.

"Spell . . . 'Bigfoot.'" He smirks.

I groan.

"Okay, what about 'alligator'?"

I groan again.

Mom takes a sip of her *café* and says, "I'm sure you'll do *fantástico*."

Despite Mom's encouragement in the morning, I'm so nervous by lunch. Lauren is sitting with us today. Ever since we ate lunch together, she joins Jenny and me a couple times a week, when she isn't reading. I'm about to ask Jenny about the spelling bee when Jessica interrupts us.

"Look, it's the weirdo twosome."

I think about what Mom said on Valentine's Day. So instead of looking up at Jessica, I pretend to ignore her. My heart is racing, but I just look forward and talk to Jenny.

"What do you want to do next Saturday? My mom said we could go to the movies."

Jenny plays along. "Oooo . . . I'll bring candy then."

This makes Jessica angry. "Did you guys hear what I said? I called you weirdos."

"Did you hear something?" Jenny says, putting her hand to her ear.

"Nothing worth listening to," I reply.

"Ugh!" says Jessica as she storms out.

"Wow, what's her problem?" whispers Lauren.

We shrug, then Jenny and I give each other a quick fist bump. Then I take a big bite out of my delicious peanut butter sandwich. Secretly, I don't know if I could have been so brave without Jenny. However, I realize that Mom was right. Suddenly, I feel less nervous about the spelling bee.

The spelling bee finally happens that afternoon back in the cafeteria. I see my poster hanging on the stage. The other third-grade classes did posters too, but all the kids in my class agree mine is the best.

"Looks so good!" Michelle gives me a high five. Even Stanley says so. At least I think so. I just see his mouth move and I begin to turn away, but then I remember him turning *roja* on Valentine's Day. I force myself to stop and say to him, "Thanks," then turn around before he can say anything else.

Since all the classes in my grade are doing the spelling bee, Jenny is already there. I rush over to sit next to her. She is sitting next to Anna and another girl. Anna is smiling much more than any of the other times I've seen her. I know that's because the other girl has to be her best friend, Isabel. Being that happy is just what happens whenever you're near your best friend.

After I say hi to Jenny and Anna, I whisper, "Hi, Isabel," and she waves back.

I was right.

Our principal, Ms. Richards, is on stage with a microphone. She has on her dolphin pin, which she only wears on special days.

"Welcome, third graders! Today is the annual spelling bee! We're going to be doing it alphabetically, of course. We will have prizes for those who make it into the second round, and a big prize for the grand winner!"

Everyone claps. The prizes at our school are pretty awesome. Kids have won school T-shirts, dolphin-shaped pencils, and even a pizza party. I whisper to Jenny, "I hope we get a pizza party!" Jenny nods.

Ms. Richards calls all the students with a last name that starts with an A onto the stage. I start to get clammy hands and a sweaty forehead. I didn't know we had to go on stage. Trisha Abrahams heads to the microphone first.

Ms. Richards says, "Trisha. Please spell the word 'happiest.'"

Trisha looks around. Then she said, "Happiest... H...A...P...P...Y...E...S...T. Happiest."

Ms. Richards presses a buzzer, which makes a big *errrrrrrrr* noise.

"Sorry, Trisha, that's wrong. Good try! Take a seat back in the audience. Jessica Anderson, do you know?" Ms. Richards asks.

Jessica sticks out her chest and says loudly, "Yes, it's happiest... H...A...P...P...I...E...S...T. Happiest."

Ms. Richards presses another buzzer, which makes a perky *ding* noise.

She says, "*Correct!* Jessica, please take a seat on the stage."

I don't want to hear the *errrrr* noise. What if I get a word that I don't know how to spell, or, worst of all, don't know how to say?

My stomach starts to hurt. Maybe I could go to the nurse. I wish Mom didn't have to work. Some of the other kids get to go home when they go to the nurse, but Mom can only pick me up if it's an emergency. Maybe this *is* a real emergency. I mean, a stomachache could be a sign of something else that I don't even know about!

Before I can figure out my escape plan, Ms. Richards says, "Will all the children with last names beginning with D come up to the stage."

I look at Jenny and whisper, "I don't want to."

"You'll be great, Stella. You got this," she says as she pats my back.

It makes me feel a little better, but my legs feel wobbly like *flan* as I walk onto the stage.

There are two students in front of me. The lights

are so bright I can't even see what is going on. Then I hear Ms. Richards say, "Estrella Díaz, will you come up to the microphone?"

I gulp, nod my head yes, and walk up to the microphone. My hands and every part of me are shaking.

"Estrella, please spell 'disappear.'"

I freeze. I wish I could disappear. If I spell it wrong, everyone is going to laugh! I look at Ms. Bell. Then Jenny. Both are smiling at me. I feel a little bit better, but my throat is closed up like I have cotton candy stuck in there. Then I remember what Mom said. I'm stronger than I realize.

Finally I close my eyes. "Disappear. D . . ."

Ms. Richards says, "Louder, dear."

I nod. "D . . . I . . . S . . . A . . . P . . . P . . . E . . . A . . . R. Disappear."

I hear a *ding* noise! Ms. Richards says, "Correct! You get to move to the next round. Take a seat on stage."

I'm surprised. That wasn't so bad! My voice didn't sound so weird on the microphone. It sounded okay. I

sit down and wait for the next round. I actually can't wait to go again.

It takes a long time to get through the rest of the students. There are about eighty of us altogether, so there are many *ding*s and *errrrr*s. Jenny makes it through to the next round. And, of course, Stanley does, too.

The next word I have to spell is "knowledge," and I, of course, know how to spell it.

"K . . . N . . . O . . . W . . . L . . . E . . . D . . . G . . . E."

I swear the *ding* sounds just a little bit more special the second time.

I make it all the way to the third round, or the semifinals, when I misspell the word "dandelion." Honestly, hearing the *errrrr* noise wasn't so bad, especially since there were only six students left on stage with me.

I get so caught up with the spelling bee that the only way I know that I made it to the semifinals is that I get a pink ribbon with a gold star that says "semifinalist." Chris Pollard ends up winning it all with the word "gregarious." I don't even know what that means! *socialoble*

Stanley also has a pink ribbon, which is surprising. I thought he'd win it all. Maybe we're alike in some ways.

Anyway, Jenny helps me put my ribbon on as we

walk past the dolphin mural, and then we link arms. We make *ding* and *errrrr* noises to each other. "Maybe we sound like dolphins. No, better yet, robots!" I whisper to Jenny. We both giggle as we start walking like robots.

I wear my ribbon proudly the rest of the day. "I can't wait to show Mom," I say quietly to myself.

Then I say even softer, "Maybe the presentation won't be so bad." This time, I kind of believe it, too.

Chapter Sixteen

When Mom gets home from work, she makes a big deal about my spelling bee ribbon, which I don't mind. She cries, *"¡Mi bebé!"* I usually don't like it when she says "my baby" in public, but at home it makes me hug her even more.

"This calls for a celebration. How about a trip to the *biblioteca* and some frozen yogurt afterward?"

I squeal and spell, "Y...E...S." That sounds like a great night. I also squeal because I love hearing the word *biblioteca*. It's such a fun word, and I love going to the library.

Mom changes out of her suit. As soon as Nick

and I see her in her jeans and sweatshirt, we know it's time to go.

"Are you going to get any books for your project, Stella?" she asks as she grabs her car keys.

"I would like a book on starfishes. Mom, did you know that if a starfish loses an arm"—I hide one of my arms behind my back and then stick it out—"they can grow one back?!" I wiggle my hand in amazement.

She nods. "Did you know some people are as strong as starfishes?"

"What do you mean, Mom? You mean like superheroes?" I ask.

She laughs. "I just mean that some people have to go through tough things and they can bounce back. Like Frida Kahlo."

"Ohh!" Then I ask, "Who is Frida Kahlo?"

"I'll tell you more about her in the car," says Mom. "She's fascinating."

Turns out Frida Kahlo was a Mexican painter who made beautiful paintings. She was in a bus accident when she was very young and had to stay in bed for months. That's when she learned how to paint. She became one of the most famous painters ever.

"Wow!" I exclaim. Hearing about Frida makes me feel proud to be from the same country.

"We can get a book on her at the *biblioteca* tonight," Mom says as she pulls into the library parking lot.

Now, the library at school is pretty cool, but the public library near my house is *incredible*! It has three levels, and beanbag chairs in the kids' section. I like to go to the reference section and look at the huge books on marine life. They have so many pictures.

The library also has art exhibits and art contests.

One time I got third place. We had to draw a scene from our favorite book, and mine was from *James and the Giant Peach*. It was the scene where the peach gets stuck on top of the Empire State Building. I found this really cool photo of the building so I could see how to draw it and added many little seagulls. Mom framed it at home and always says that one day it will be very valuable.

When we get to the library, I see a sign near the front door that reads "Local Author Presentation in the Auditorium."

"Mom, can we go, *por favor*?" I ask. If I say please, Mom usually says yes.

Mom looks at her watch and then at me. I'm giving her the biggest puppy-dog eyes I can. She nods yes and gives me a kiss on the head.

Nick says, "It starts in thirty minutes. Time to move it," as he runs over to the graphic novels.

In the meantime, I spot more books on marine animals while Mom looks for a book on Frida Kahlo and some mystery novels for herself.

Since I've already done research at the library for my project, I know exactly where the fish books are. I only have a few more fishes to go, and I also want to get more photos for the starfish page that I am finishing. I find a picture of a royal starfish that's purple with an orange border.

Nick wanders over with a stack of graphic novels and peeks over my shoulder.

"I can't wait to draw it!" I whisper.

"I'm sure it will be great like the rest of your drawings, little Miss Frida Kahlo."

I giggle. "Do you think they'll have one at the Shedd Aquarium?"

Nick shrugs his shoulders. "Maybe. Also Mom's a little busy with work, so I don't know when exactly we will go."

Nick's been so great about the presentation. He told Mom about the Shedd Aquarium idea, and now I just hope we really can go. We've also been brainstorming how to make my presentation more interesting, and he suggested that I should be a fisherman. That sounds a little boring, but then I came up with the idea of doing a submarine. I just need to finish my research before I start building it.

Nick says, "Come on, champ. Time to go!"

I grab his arm and we run over to Mom, who is standing near the auditorium.

We enter just as the show is starting. Not only is it an author, but it's a children's book author and a girl! She starts the presentation by reading out loud a few of her books. One of them is even in English and Spanish. How cool is that! Obviously, I understand both parts. Later she speaks about how she got started as an author. She grew up in Texas like Stanley. Turns out she had problems speaking as a kid, just like me. She would switch the letters around. Everyone thought she wasn't really smart. Because of that, she read even more and made herself write all the time. Then she decided that's what she wanted to do when she grew up.

I whisper to Mom, "She's a starfish."

She puts her arm around me and kisses me on top of the head. Then I realize that maybe I'm a starfish, too. My name is Estrella, after all.

When I get home, I draw the royal starfish. As soon as I'm done, I whisper to Pancho, "Don't tell anyone, but I might want to be an author one day."

Pancho, of course, doesn't say anything. He's the best at keeping secrets.

Chapter Seventeen

I'm in the middle of reading about narwhals when Dad picks us up. The narwhal is a type of whale. People think it has a giant tusk, but it's actually a tooth. Narwhals are extra special because they are rarely seen. People tried to keep them in captivity in the 1960s and 1970s, but sadly they kept dying.

I only see Dad once or twice a year, and this time it's right before spring break. He's in Chicago for a week with my Tío Carlos.

Apparently, they are going to some sort of convention for my *tío*'s clothing store.

When Dad arrives at our house, he is in a new car that I've never seen before. Dad always likes to drive instead of flying, so he must have gotten it back in Colorado. The new car is a sports car. You know, the ones that look like they go really fast. I'm used to this, though. Every time I see him, it's a new car. As we put on our seat belts, he says that he's taking Nick and me bowling.

"Cool!" says Nick.

I don't say anything. I've never been bowling before. I'm excited, but I don't know what to expect.

As soon as we get to the bowling alley, Dad says to us, "You guys paying?" He laughs.

I look over to Nick. He's not laughing. I know why, too. Since Dad never sends us money, we never know when he will actually pay for things. Mom knows this, so she always gives us extra money when we see him just in case he makes us pay.

"Nick, it's just a joke."

Nick is still not laughing. Dad just shrugs. He goes over to the register.

"One adult and two kids."

Dad opens up his wallet. I see a picture of Nick when he was little. Then I see a picture of a baby.

"Who's that?" I ask, pointing to the picture.

"You!" he says.

I'm a little surprised.

"Really?"

"*Sí*, it's you, from your first passport picture before we moved to the United States. *Vamos*, let's get some *zapatos* on your feet!"

Apparently, you can't wear regular shoes on the bowling lanes. You have to borrow these really cool shoes that are colorful.

I put them on. "I think I might like bowling," I say to Nick. I kick my heels together like Dorothy in *The Wizard of Oz*.

"Let's go, Twinkle Toes," Nick says.

We walk over to the lanes, and Dad enters our

names into the computer. Then he hands me a few different balls to find one that I can bowl with. I find a bright orange one that I can actually carry.

"*Señoritas primero,*" says Dad. I like it when Dad says, "Girls go first." Nick blows a raspberry.

I'm all smiles until I walk toward the lane. The floor is slippery, and I get all nervous trying to lift the ball. It feels too heavy.

"What do I do, Dad?" I ask.

"It's not rocket science. Just roll the ball," says Nick.

I turn *roja*, this time because I'm angry. Just because I'm new to something doesn't mean I'm stupid. I wish that I were a narwhal right now so I could poke Nick with my giant tooth. Instead, I stick my tongue out at Nick. Then I roll the ball. It goes nowhere near the white pins.

In fact, my first two balls go right into the gutter. Nick goes next. He is much better than me and knocks a few pins over. Dad is really good. He knocks over all the pins. I don't know much about bowling, but he kicks out his leg like the professionals.

"Dad, how come you are so good?" I ask.

"Well, I used to go bowling a bunch when I was a teenager." He reties his shoe and looks at me. "I wasn't very close to my parents. They were more concerned with their parties than with your *tío* or me. Once I no longer had a *nana*, a nanny, I spent all my time with my friends bowling or playing pool."

I feel sad for a second. I never thought about Dad as a kid. It sounds kind of lonely. I love spending time with Mom and Nick.

I look at him. I say in Spanish, "Dad, could you teach me how to bowl better?"

"Claro que sí, mi amor, Stella." "Of course, my love," he says.

He shows me how to line up my feet with these

little arrows first. Next he shows me how to swing my arm better and finally to let the ball roll. When I do it by myself, the ball goes slower than it did before, but it's going straight down the middle. I actually knock over some pins. Almost all of them!

"Way to go, Stella!" says Nick. He gives me a high five.

Dad kisses the top of my head. I smile. For a moment, I miss having him around.

After we finish bowling, Dad drops us off at the house.

"Before you go . . ." he says, grabbing a box from the back seat. "Here are new coats for the two of you."

I see the tags. They are from my *tío*'s store. Dad gives Nick and me each a coat. I try mine on. It's too big. It's also pink, with fur. I like pink, but a whole pink coat is too girly for me. Still I say, *"Gracias."*

I look over at Nick, and I giggle. His coat is way too small. It's so tight around his shoulders he can't even put down his arms.

"Oh, I guess you grew more than I realized. You're going to be as tall as your uncle!" Nick just shrugs and hands him back the coat.

"I'll mail you a new one," Dad says.

Nick looks at me. We both know that is never going to happen.

I give Dad a hug goodbye. I feel a little sad again. My dad is not all terrible. He just doesn't know better. It's like the people who used to hunt narwhals. People used to think that narwhals were related to unicorns. They didn't know they were regular sea mammals and weren't magical. I think part of Dad just doesn't realize he's not doing a good job at being a father. Then again, I don't think he knows how. It doesn't sound like he had really great parents. Nick and I are lucky because at least we have Mom.

Nick puts his arm around me as we go back inside our house. As we open the door, I smell something wonderful. Mom is in the kitchen making *albóndigas* again. I run into the kitchen and hug her tightly around the waist.

"Whoa, Stella! You surprised me."

I look up at her. "I love you, Mommy."

"I love you more," she says as she hugs me back.

Chapter Eighteen

Today, I turn nine years old, which means I'm big enough to take more care of myself.

This year my birthday is on a Saturday, so I don't have to go to school. Good thing, too, because I couldn't sleep last night thinking about the day ahead. Mom pretended not to remember my birthday last night when we were playing games and eating Chinese food.

"Mom, are we doing anything special tomorrow?" I asked.

"I'm not sure. Should we?" she said with a wink.

"Yeah, nothing special happens tomorrow. The

most boring day ever," said Nick. I stuck my tongue out at him and opened my fortune cookie.

I went to sleep a little worried, but I was pretty sure I could hear presents being wrapped and smell cake being baked in the kitchen in the middle of the night.

So when I hear Mom tiptoeing into my room and I see lighted candles, I know she and Nick didn't forget. They sing "Happy Birthday" twice. The first time in English and the second time in Spanish. I blow out all nine candles at the same time and feel extra lucky.

On our birthdays, we always get to eat cake for breakfast. Mom made my favorite this year—coconut cake with a special type of caramel called *cajeta*. Then she put a bunch of sliced mangoes on top. I run to the kitchen to grab the plates while Mom and Nick chase after me.

When I get to the kitchen, I see wrapped presents on the table. There's even one for Nick because Mom always says that we need to celebrate being *hermano* and *hermana*. Because I'm a really good *hermana*, I let him open his present first.

But before that, I give him a card I made that has a drawing of a sea dragon on it. Sea dragons are like sea horses, but they look like leafy dragons. Inside it says, "To the best big *hermano*! Love, Stella."

I drew the sea dragon because if my brother were a fish, he'd be a sea dragon. He always takes care of me like the male sea dragons do. Sea dragons also carry their young on their tails. Nick still gives me piggyback rides sometimes. Plus, Nick really likes dragons in general. It's the only animal he draws.

"Thanks, sis!"

Mom says, "*Ahora* it's Stella's turn!"

I squeal and open up my four presents on the table, one at a time. The first is an envelope, and inside are tickets for the Shedd Aquarium!

"This is going to help me finish my fish project!" I say. "Thanks, Mom!"

"Way to go, Mom!" Nick cheers.

Then I open the second present. *James and the Giant Peach*!

"Now you don't have to check it out from the library anymore," Mom says.

"*¡Gracias!*" I say.

I jump up to hug her and she kisses my cheek. Mom is the best. She used to try to give me baby dolls, but then she realized that I like books and art supplies way more.

The third present is a bigger box. It's 128 colored

pencils, the fancy artist kind! Before I only had twenty-four. I also didn't have any of the metallic colors. Now, I'll be able to draw superheroes with metallic capes for my brother. I saw Stanley doing that at school the other day, and it looked really cool.

"You can use the metallic ones to draw details on your submarine!" says Nick.

We high-five. He's so smart.

The last present is really small, like the size of a note. I open it. It's a card. On the front it says "To *la mejor hija*," or "to the best daughter."

I open the card. Written inside is "Go to the garage."

"It's a surprise!" I yell as I run into the garage. "I love surprises!"

There, in the middle of the garage, is a red bicycle—without training wheels! Mom and Nick like to go riding with each other around the neighborhood on the weekends. I was always a little jealous, but I didn't have a bike without training wheels, so I would play at Jenny's instead.

"Awesome!" I say as I jump up and down. "Can we ride now?"

"No riding until you eat your cake for breakfast." Mom winks.

"Deal!" We all shake hands on it.

After two slices of cake, I put on my outdoor clothes and grab my helmet. I want to wear my pajamas, but Mom doesn't think that is a good idea. "Stella, the robe will get stuck in the wheels," she warns.

The three of us walk our bikes to the park across the street to practice.

I put on my helmet. "I'm ready!"

I put one foot on a pedal. The bike starts wobbling. I try to put my other foot on the other pedal. It wobbles even more. This is *much* harder than when I used to ride with training wheels. What if I fall? Then I look around. Worse, what if someone sees?

I look at Nick and whisper, "This is scary."

Nick walks over and holds the bike. "It's okay, kiddo. Get both feet on the pedals."

I do and he holds the bike.

"Okay, now just pedal."

I try, but I stop and put my feet on the ground. "Mom, what if I fall?" My lip is starting to shake.

Mom walks over, and both of them look at me. "Everyone falls at some point, Stella."

"Yeah, I'm pretty much the best at everything, but even I fell a little bit at the beginning," says Nick. Then he rubs my helmet.

"Really?"

"But . . . *mi chiquitita*, Stella, if you don't want to ride you don't have to today," Mom says. "It's your birthday and it's Stella's rules."

"Yeah, we can play video games. And I'll let you beat me." Nick elbows me gently.

I take a deep breath. It takes all of my courage, but I say, "No, I'll try. I am stronger than I think. Right, Mom?"

Mom nods.

It takes about ten tries with Nick holding the bike while I get started. Like the sea dragon, he knows when to let go so I can swim away on my own. Finally, I ride the bike a few times without any help. Before I know it, I'm doing loops around the playground with Mom and Nick. Each loop feels more natural and my legs get less shaky. They start to feel strong.

As I ride around, I can't help but imagine all the fun times I'll have riding my bike now with Nick and Jenny. I wonder if Anna knows how to ride a bike. Maybe all of us could ride together. That makes me feel excited and I begin to pedal faster. Then I wonder if Stanley knows how to ride a bike. I'm sure he'd be really good at it, but then again I'm not sure anymore. Stanley's not always the best at everything, just the best at most things. For a brief second, I imagine Stanley riding bikes with us and I pedal faster and faster.

Chapter Nineteen

"Wow!" I say as we walk through the big doors of the Shedd Aquarium. My mouth drops open. It's more beautiful than I imagined, with giant columns and chandeliers hanging everywhere.

I am so happy to finally be visiting the aquarium. I know it will help me finish my project. I've nearly completed all the drawings, and started the submarine, but I need a little extra inspiration to figure out what I'm going to say. I'm still pretty nervous about it, but Nick promises he'll help me practice.

"This is so exciting I could spell!" I say, then I spell, "E...X...C...I...T...I...N...G."

Nick rolls his eyes. "Come on, Bumblebee."

I grab a map right away and start trying to figure out where everything is. I especially want to make sure to see the lionfish since it's the last fish in my animal project. Lionfish are origi-nally from the Indian Ocean and the Pacific Ocean, but many aquariums have them on display, including the Shedd Aquarium.

As we wait in line to enter the exhibits, I look all around at the signs hanging from the ceiling. The aquarium is so big, and it's full of so many people! There's an area for people to check coats, an area with tour guides, and a really long line to get tickets.

Luckily, Mom has the tickets already, so we can go right in to see the exhibits.

"Ready?" asks Mom. I nod and I lead my family to the jellyfish room.

When we enter the dark room, there is a soft glow, but as we walk toward the glass, it grows brighter. It's like magic. We spend a bunch of time looking at the different types of jellyfish and trying to decide which one is our favorite.

"Did you know they don't have brains?" I say.

"That's cool!" Nick replies.

After the jellyfish, we walk to the Amazon Rising section, where it's humid and warm. That's because there are more than just fishes in this section. It's a mini jungle filled with plants and other Amazonian creatures such as tarantulas, monkeys, and even an anaconda! Out of the fishes in the Amazon, Mom likes the leopard whipray and zebra-striped stingrays best, while I like the fruit-eating fish named the tambaqui. Nick makes us stop at his favorite, the piranha exhibit.

"Be careful, Stella. I hear they especially like to eat nine-year-old girls."

I roll my eyes. "Can we go see the sea dragons next?" Mom and Nick agree with me. But just as we walk into the sea dragon area, I see a familiar boy with light-brown hair holding a map in front of his face. As soon as he lowers it, I know who it is.

Stanley.

Stanley Mason.

I whisper to myself, "Really, why is he here?"

I grab my map and lift it in front of my face. Even though I feel a tiny bit less nervous around him now, I'm not ready to talk to him outside of school. *"¡Rápido!"* I think. Immediately, I plan my escape. "Oh, I meant sea turtles!" I start walking into another hallway.

Mom and Nick look at each other. "Whatever you want, Stella."

When we get to the sea turtles, I don't see Stanley. I relax and watch the sea turtles gracefully swim. It's almost as if they are doing tai chi. Except instead of doing it outside in the park like my neighbors do, the sea turtles are doing it in the water.

Then I hear Stanley shout, "Awesome!"

I whisper to Mom, "There're too many people in here. Let's go see the sea otters *now*." I walk even faster this time.

My *roja* quickly goes away when we enter the sea otter room. Straightaway, I know this is my favorite room and it's not just because it feels cooler. The sea otters might be the Olympic gymnasts of the sea. They spin, twirl, and flip through the water all while looking adorable. I desperately want to get a better look at one, so I chase it around the curved tank. But as I go around the curve, I almost run right into Stanley! He's too busy looking at another sea otter with his dad to notice though. This time, I don't even wait to say anything to Mom or Nick. I just run into the next room.

"Wait!" Nick and Mom both say as they chase after me.

The rest of the day goes like that. Instead of seeing dolphins, sharks, and even penguins, I see Stanley, Stanley, and Stanley.

"Why don't we take a break?" Mom says. I can tell she is a little tired and annoyed from running all around.

We go to the cafeteria, and I order two scoops of lime sherbet with nuts on top. It doesn't help. My perfect day at the aquarium is nothing like I had hoped it would be. Worst of all, I am too embarrassed to tell Mom and Nick why I was running from room to room.

Mom can tell something is bothering me. *"¿Stella, todo está bien?"* She's asking me if everything is okay. She only speaks pure Spanish to me when it's something serious.

"Sí, the aquarium is very big. I'm just tired." I rest my face on the table.

"Stella, did I see that boy Stanley from your class?" Mom asks.

"No." I keep my head on the table. If she could see my face, she'd know I was lying. I don't like lying to Mom, but I'm too embarrassed to tell her the truth.

"My mistake." I feel her hand on my head. She

starts making a braid with my hair, and I feel a little better.

"Well, we can go then and come back another time, but why don't we get you a small birthday *regalo*?"

I lift my head. Another *regalo*, another present! When we enter the museum store, I know what I want right away. Under the giant octopus in the middle of the store is a huge, beautiful book with the title *The Ultimate Guide to Sea Creatures* in glittery letters. It's filled with so many pictures that I want to draw. I hug the book, close my eyes, and spell, "A . . . W . . . E . . . S . . . O . . . M . . . E!"

I open my eyes and hear a voice that says, "It *is* awesome!"

It is Stanley. I want to run, but I can't. Mom and Nick are a few feet away. If I sprint out of the store, they'll think something is very wrong, instead of the truth, which is that I'm just too shy to talk to Stanley. Then I notice that Stanley is holding the same book. Suddenly, I remember what Jenny told me. Just ask questions. Be Sherlock Holmes. Using my own power of deduction, I realize I have something to say. It's the perfect question. I mean, he's at the aquarium, he said the book was awesome. So I take a deep breath. My throat is dry, but I manage to ask quietly, "Do you like marine life, Stanley?"

"Y . . . U . . . P!" Stanley spells. He opens *The Ultimate Guide to Sea Creatures* and points to the lionfish in the book. "This one is my favorite."

"That's one of my favorites, too!" I say. "It's actually the last fish in my animal project."

"Cool!" says Stanley. "You know, I was going to do fishes, too, but I saw your drawings and realized mine would never be as good. So I decided to do monkeys instead. I'm doing a monkey mobile."

He grins. I'm surprised. He saw my project? I never thought he'd be interested in what I was doing.

Stanley says, "I've been wanting to talk to you about your drawings and how you got so good, but I thought you didn't like me. You always cover up your drawings and turn away before I can ask you."

"That's not true at all!" I quickly reply. "I also have some art books if you want to see them. I draw from them all the time."

"Yeah!" he says. "That'd be awesome!"

Stanley then opens his book and starts pointing out all his favorite fish. I start doing the same. Before I know it I'm no longer *roja* and I don't have to think about what I am going to say. Talking to Stanley feels normal, like talking to Nick or Jenny.

I ask him, "Stanley, do you know what you are doing for your presentation?"

"I'm going to wear an ape costume! What about you?"

"Not sure yet."

"You should dress up like Jacques Cousteau!"

I gasp. That is the best idea.

"I really need to come up with something else to go with my ape costume though. It's not like I can bribe people with cookies again."

"What do you mean?" I can feel my eyebrows pushing together.

"I give out cookies every time I'm new or trying to get people to like me. That's a trick my mom taught me."

I giggle, remembering Stanley's birthday cookies. I can't believe he was nervous then. He looked as cool as a cucumber.

"Moms are the best," I say.

Then Stanley's dad walks over and says, "Who is this, buddy?" He's grinning and has a Texas accent.

"Oh, this is Stella. Stella is in my class and she loves fishes, too. She's an expert at math and spelling and is the class artist."

I beam. "Fishes are simply...A...M...A...Z...I...N...G."

Stanley's dad says, "Well, she seems like a great friend! You guys should play together. You've been looking for a friend to ride bikes with since we moved here. Do you know how to ride a bike, Stella?"

Nick walks over. "Stella is great at riding bikes." He squeezes my shoulder. Then he whispers into my ear, "We'll practice more."

Mom links arms with me. "Hi, Stanley." I look up at her slowly. I'm a little nervous that she might be upset with me for lying, but instead of a frown, she has a giant smile. She winks at me. "I don't know about you all, but I'm starving. Who wants pizza?"

Nick and I raise our hands.

"Stanley, would you and your father like to join us?"

"Can we, Dad?" exclaims Stanley.

"Sure! We've been meaning to try real Chicago deep-dish pizza!" he replies.

"Mom, do you mind if we see the lionfish before we go?" I ask. "It's the last fish in my project. I accidentally forgot to see it earlier."

Mom nods, and the five of us walk to the lionfish.

While they might be in one of the smaller tanks, the lionfish do not disappoint. They are more lovely in real life.

"Wow, they move so slowly," says Stanley, pointing at a white-and-black lionfish.

I nod and say, "I wonder if it's because of their shape. They almost look like peacocks!"

Stanley grins in agreement. The lionfish have large striped rays that spread out all around them.

"Well, they don't look too happy," replies Nick.

I giggle. The lionfish do look like they're pouting.

"Maybe they're hungry? Did you know lionfish can go up to three months without eating?" I say.

"Cool!" says Stanley.

"I don't know about you guys, but I'm not a lionfish," says Nick. "Let's go get some pizza."

Everyone laughs and we head to the pizzeria. Over delicious messy deep-dish, we talk and look at my new book at the table. I have to clean my hands and face con-  stantly with my napkin, but I don't mind. I like being able to share my new present with everyone. As I wipe tomato sauce off my face for the millionth time, I smile. My new book is a top-notch present, but how the day ended is probably the best present of all.

Chapter Twenty

When I wake up on the day of the presentation, I feel mostly happy about going to school. It might be the fact that I'm nine now or that the school year is almost over, but lately things have been good. I did well in the spelling bee, I can ride a bike, and Jessica isn't really bothering me anymore.

It's not like Jessica hasn't tried. I've just become a professional at ignoring her. Having more friends helps, too. It means I'm not alone in dealing with Jessica, and she's less likely to say something. Lunch is also more fun because Lauren, Isabel, and Anna eat with Jenny and me more regularly. I even sometimes talk to Lauren in class now, although we both still like being quiet. I don't run away from Stanley anymore, and I'm not afraid he thinks I'm weird, because we're friends now.

Best of all, I am ready for my presentation. I'm going to dress up like Jacques Cousteau, like Stanley suggested, which goes perfectly with my submarine. I made it out of Styrofoam poster board and glued my fish drawings on the outside. Both Jenny and Stanley helped. Jenny cut out all the fishes perfectly while Stanley helped with making sure the submarine was realistic-looking.

"Real submarines have portholes," said Stanley. "And nuclear reactors!"

"I think I'll skip the nuclear reactor," I replied.

As promised, Nick helped me practice the presentation the night before.

"You don't want to memorize the whole presentation. It sounds lame. Also, you don't want to read from a handout. That makes it so boring."

So we practiced the first minute, when I introduce myself as Jacques Cousteau. With Nick's help, I came up with the best introduction. It was so good that I presented it to Mom.

"My name is Jacques Cousteau. Welcome to the wonderful world of fishes! Have you ever wondered what lives in the sea? Well, today I'm going to tell you!"

Mom applauded.

Over our morning cereal, Nick gives me a little pep talk. "Remember the first minute is the hardest. Then it's easy peasy."

"Lemon squeezy," I reply.

"That's right, Mr. Cousteau." He shakes my hand.

I wish Nick could go with me to school. Luckily, Mom is able to come for the presentation. She wanted to help me set up the submarine, and we also have an appointment before class with Ms.

Thompson about my speech progress. As we walk up to the building, I see a boy in an ape costume. I wave.

"H...E...L...L...O, Stanley."

"Hi, S...T...E...L...L...A!"

I'm a little nervous when Mom meets with Ms. Thompson. I think I'm doing better in speech, but I can never tell. I sit outside her office while they talk before my class. After a few minutes, both Mom and Ms. Thompson come back outside. Mom is smiling. Ms. Thompson says, "That's an interesting outfit, Stella." She seems a little confused as she looks at my blue turtleneck, blue pants, and red beanie.

"I'm Jacques Cousteau!"

She laughs. "Oh, of course!" Then she continues, "Stella, I'm sad to say that I think this is goodbye for us. I recommended to your mom that you stop taking speech classes."

I squeal. I'm so happy.

"But I want you to read out loud at night for practice."

"I promise."

"Take care, Stella," she says.

I wave goodbye. As we walk to class, Mom whispers, "Can you believe she still asked me if your father is moving back?"

I am definitely glad not to be answering that question anymore.

When we get to the classroom, we set up my submarine. Mom can't stay the whole day because she has to work, which means I have to go first with my presentation.

"You'll feel better getting it done sooner, too," Mom whispers. To shake off the nerves, we do some jumping jacks.

I notice Jessica staring at us. She's wearing an equestrian outfit for her presentation.

"Good luck with your presentation, Jessica," says Mom.

Jessica crosses her arms and turns around. I look up at Mom, who pats my head. She's the best.

I walk to the front of the class.

I feel myself turning *roja* when I first open my mouth. My turtleneck feels *apretado* around my neck, like a boa constrictor.

"Hello . . ."

My voice is shaky.

"My name is . . ."

"Louder," someone says.

I catch eyes with Jessica, who looks very smug. I can only imagine what she's thinking. I start doubting myself, but then I look out to the crowd. On my left, I see Stanley in his ape costume. He gives me the thumbs-up.

"My name is Jacques Cousteau," I say without my voice shaking.

I look out to the crowd again. This time I notice Ms. Bell, who is in the middle and smiling.

I take a deep breath. I stick out my chest.

"Welcome to the wonderful world of fishes!"

When I look out to my right, I see that Mom's taking pictures. Surrounded by my support system, my inner starfish starts taking over.

"Have you ever wanted to know what lives in the sea?" I see Ben, Lauren, and a bunch of kids nod their heads. "Well, today I'm going to tell you!"

As usual, Nick was right about the first minute. It does get much easier! I point out all nineteen fishes on my submarine. I made more fishes than I had to for the project. With fishes with names like blobfish and wahoo, I just couldn't help it. I get excited the more and more I talk, and when I'm done people actually applaud! I immediately run to the back to hug Mom.

"*Fantástico, Stella,*" she whispers. She stays to watch Stanley's presentation, which is pretty great, too.

Stanley uses monkeys from the Barrel of Monkeys game to make a mobile and printed out facts about monkeys on banana shapes. Plus, he is really funny in his ape costume. He even makes monkey noises. I clap loudly for him when he finishes. He certainly didn't need the cookies.

Lauren's presentation is also good. She brought in her uncle's parrot like she said she would. But it turns out the parrot doesn't talk, he just whistles. She still has to talk the whole time, so I make sure to smile and give her the thumbs-up while she presents.

Jessica's presentation is the most boring. She reads her presentation from her notebook and just flips through a slideshow of different horses. Like usual, Jessica doesn't seem nervous at all, but I realize maybe that's not always good. Maybe it's good sometimes to be nervous about things because you'll work harder at them.

At the end of the school day, Ms. Bell hands us our grades on our projects. She gives me three gold stars and an A plus plus plus. She also wrote *Wahoo,* like the fish I mentioned during my presentation, on top, next to a smiley face.

I grab my cheeks because my face hurts from smiling so much. I just can't stop! Not only did I speak out loud in front of the whole class, I did it well. Today, I really lived up to my name. I really was an Estrella.

Chapter Twenty-One

Even though it's summer and we've finished our animal projects, I still like reading about marine life. My new favorite is the sea otter, mostly because I loved seeing several of them at the Shedd. It also doesn't hurt that they look like teddy bears with thick, soft fur. While researching them, I found out that when they sleep, they hold on to each other's paws so they have someone to protect them.

I'm too old to hold hands, but if I were a sea otter I would have many people to hold paws with. I'd hold paws with Nick, Mom, Jenny, and my family in Mexico. I even think Stanley and I would be sea otter *amigos*. Jenny and I are also talking about doing a sleepover with Anna and Isabel. I've never done a sleepover that big before.

For me, summer doesn't officially start until my family walks to Oberweis to get ice cream. Of course we could drive there, but walking is more of an adventure. We pass through different neighborhoods where there are all types of houses. There are gingerbread-looking houses, big houses, and houses with pools. I like to imagine how different my life would be if we lived in one of those big houses. Then I look at Mom and Nick and I don't want anything else. Our favorite game to play as we walk is spies. Mom always starts us off.

"Okay, *niños*. Where is our big mission?"

"Russia," I say. In all the spy movies, they are in Russia.

"Oh, good one!" says Nick. "I'll be Boris."

"Call me Natasha," I say.

Mom laughs. Then we pretend we're being chased. We run in between houses, and Nick tells the dogs to be quiet while we tiptoe. By the time we get to Oberweis, we're dying for ice cream.

I usually order lime sherbet with nuts, but today I want to try something different. I go with strawberry frozen yogurt with gummy bears. Nick always gets cookies and cream. Mom is crazy though. She likes to switch around. Sometimes it's coffee, butter pecan, or chocolate. She puts her hand to her chin, pauses, looks at me, and says, "What do I look like?"

"Without a doubt, butter pecan," I answer.

Nick rolls his eyes. "Why do I have to live with two *loca* ladies?"

"We're not crazy, we're just creative," I reply while crossing my arms. Then I put two little fingers above my head like an alien. Nick ruffles my hair.

After our ice cream adventure, I meet up with

Stanley and Jenny to ride bikes around the parking lot at the school.

"Stella, can you ride your bike without holding the handlebars?" asks Stanley.

"That's scary!" I exclaim.

Stanley and Jenny raise their arms for a second and howl.

"It's," Stanley says, " F . . . U . . . N."

Jenny agrees. "Try it, Stella."

I feel sweaty as I lift up one arm and then the other. My arms are shaking, but it feels a little less scary than I thought.

I let out a small howl. It feels great!

I raise my arms higher above my head. Then Stanley and Jenny join me, and the three of us howl together.

Author's Note

Stella Díaz Has Something to Say is based on my childhood. How much is true? Well, if I had to say, it's 82.9 percent true, to be exact.

Like Stella I struggled with my English and Spanish, took speech classes for three years, and had a Vietnamese best friend. I had a pretty good older brother, a fun mother, and a not-so-great dad. I was also born in Mexico and loved the library. I did not grow up near Chicago, but I just love the Shedd Aquarium. It's my favorite aquarium. My brother's name is Alejandro, not Nick, and my best friend's name is Mimi, not Jenny. I do love fishes, but not as much as Stella does. The biggest difference between Stella and me is, unlike Stella, I love coffee and do not think it is gross at all.

I wrote *Stella Díaz Has Something to Say* to share some of the wonderful memories of my childhood, but also to share some of the challenges of being different and the frustrations of being misunderstood. Like Stella, it took me a while to realize people are just people even if they seem cooler, smarter, or more interesting than you. You never know until you talk to them.

More than anything, I hope that after reading *Stella Díaz Has Something to Say*, you might discover your own inner starfish. I know I did. Stella gave me the motivation to take Spanish classes and finally begin to feel comfortable with the language. Never forget that you're so much stronger than you realize. You'll be surprised by what you can accomplish.

Acknowledgments

I've always loved reading the acknowledgments in books. They are little windows into how a book was created. But mostly I read them hoping that, maybe one day, I'd be able to write my own.

Well, amazingly, here I am writing them for the first time—and hopefully not the last!

First, I'd like to acknowledge my dear friend Erika Lutz for reviewing the first drafts of this book when it was a picture-book dummy and for reading all my early stories back in San Francisco. She's one of those people you can always count on, and for that she'll be a lifelong friend. Second, I'd like to thank Linda Pratt, my literary agent. She gave me the confidence to return to my cast-aside picture-book idea about a shy girl named Stella and turn it into a chapter book. Without her and her priceless feedback, I'm not sure if I would have ever taken the plunge.

Then I'd like to thank my amazing, extraordinary editor, Connie Hsu. I have to admit I was overwhelmed when she first suggested my story needed to be at least three times longer, but I'm eternally grateful she did. Thank you for working with me for nine months before the book was even under contract, and for all your guidance afterward, too. This book wouldn't exist without you. Huge thanks to everyone at Roaring Brook, especially Kristie Radwilowicz, Elizabeth Holden Clark, Aimee Fleck, and Megan Abbate. A big shout-out to Ruth Chan and Eda Kaban for reading nearly every draft of the story (and there were many). Also, I have to thank my boyfriend, Kyle, for making me *albóndigas* and for his support while I worked on the final art.

I must thank the following people who helped inspire this story: my lovable big brother, Alejandro, Chris Pollard, Mimi Le, Anna Gonzalez, Isabel Roxas, my father, my teachers, and all the real-life Stanley Masons who made me turn *roja*.

Last, the biggest thank-you goes to my mom. Thank you, Mom, for always believing in me, for reading every single draft, and for your strength, inspiration, and continued support. I love you more than I love *albóndigas*, and, as you know, that means a lot.